A Promise of Peaches

Also by Valerie Volk

In Due Season (Pantaenus Press, 2009)

Valerie Volk

A Promise of Peaches

Acknowledgements

I am indebted to many people who have commented on this verse novel during and after the writing process. Some of these gave invaluable help with research, and told me of their experiences as immigrants to Australia in the 1940s and 1950s. Members of the Czech community in Adelaide have been especially helpful. Others have read and given helpful feedback on the book while or after it was written. Because all these have contributed so much to the finished product, I am naming them in alphabetical order, with my grateful thanks: Jude Aquilina, Claire Bell, Greta and Ian Bird, Ute Buettner, Bruce Dawe, Eddie Dubsky, Yr Ham, Trevor Hampel, Alison Hastie, Rosanne Hawke, Sue Jenkins, Geoff Page, Ioana Petrescu, Thomas Shapcott, Ute Slizys, Miroslav Stibr, Felicity Volk, Caz Williams, Mark Worthing, the staff at the South Australian Migration Museum and the members of my two writing groups, Literati and Poetica.

There are three people to whom I am especially indebted: Anne Jantzen, an ever encouraging and responsive reader, Stephen Matthews of Ginninderra Press for his belief in this book, and David Harris, always my rock and support.

A Promise of Peaches
ISBN 978 1 74027 656 6
Copyright © text Valerie Volk 2010

First published 2010
Reprinted 2017

GINNINDERRA PRESS
PO Box 3461 Port Adelaide 5015
www.ginninderrapress.com.au

Contents

For my parents, who are not Doss and Joe, but who had the same generosity of heart and kindliness to anyone in need.

Claire, 2009

On the wall – up there –
Look! Do you see them?
Golden globules, like small suns,
that moment when the sun has tipped the hills
to chase the shadows of the night away.

Come on, girl. Don't be scared.
Don't look at me like that!
I may be old, but I'm not senile yet.
I tell you there are peaches on the wall.

Yes, that's the way. Look higher still.
Just underneath the ceiling, yellow balls.
Aha, you've found them now.
At least it's wiped that patient smile,
that condescending look, from your smug face.

Of all the nurses – 'carers' you prefer –
you are the one who most annoys me.
You with your cow-like eyes, the fluttering hands,
your eager efforts to engage my mind.
As if I'd waste my mind on one like you.

And I can hear you in the staffroom, so demure:
'I think I'm making headway.
Today she smiled at me.'
Or are you far more honest?
'Today the old witch bared her fangs!'
Beneath that bovine Pollyanna surface
are you much more aware than I give credit for?
Perhaps you even see in me the things I seek to hide
lest showing others further disempowers me.

But now you turn that stupid smile on me
and ask me why I call them peaches.
Well clearly, child, because it's what they look like –
like golden peaches hanging on the wall.
I swear if you begin to tell me that it's just
refracted light that comes with early sunbeams
through ventilation grids above my head
I'll scream abuse to send you running from the room.
I have forgotten more of physics than you ever knew.

It doesn't matter. Now I watch them as they lessen;
the sun moves upward through the sky – their fullness fades,
reduces. First three-quarters, then a half,
and now a quarter circle. Soon they will be gone.
Soon all will go.

Claire, 2009

'It was my father taught me they were peaches.
A fancy for the child I was. My bedroom in that house
had such a grid above my head, and just like this
I lay and watched them grow and die.'

Why do I tell you this? As if you care!

'Go on, girl, you can go!
I'll call you when I need you. Yes, I can reach the bell.
No, it's not bad. The pain's surmountable,
and if it's not, I'll deal with it myself.
Your presence adds insult to injury.
I've never willingly shown weakness, and
not to such as you. Just go.'

Claire, 2009

The blest relief of solitude. Of all the huge indignities
that age enforces, this is worst –
the powerlessness that it brings.
The incapacity to say 'Thus far, no more.'
Dictate to others 'This I will, but that is all.
No further.'

Eager hands smoothing bedclothes that,
in sheer perversity, I rumple as they leave the room.
Food I have not chosen; of course I will not eat for them.
The kind forbearance that's more maddening
than outright cruelty.
Benevolent dictatorships that tell me Eat! Excrete! and
cannot understand why I should cringe when probed with
questions that intrude upon my privacy. The movement of my bowels?
My business only. They insist that it is theirs. A trip outside?
I'll do that when I want, not when you tell me. How's that foot?
So in defiance I stomp corridors and bear the agony.

The only privacy is in my mind. There I retreat
to tread the halls of memory. Sometimes a comfort,
others only misery. But always questions, questions…

Claire, 2009

I would not show her, but I felt my breathing alter,
when we talked of peaches on the wall.
An old familiar sickness, the gorge rising,
as memories began to swim their tortuous way
up through the murk of years, groping slowly, slowly,
to the surface of my mind.

I see myself, the paddler in the boat,
reaching desperately, with oar upraised,
seeking only power to beat them down.
But they are slippery devils, eel-like
they slither underneath my craft, and rise again
to face me mockingly the other side.
And I am tired. Too tired to keep fighting.
Let them come, their faces taking shape,
rising and falling through the muddied waters,
floating corpse-like, bloated, on the surface,
asking to be dragged aboard, to join me
on this final voyage.

So can I still refuse them place?

Claire, 2009/Clara, 1942

Another room. Another sunny morning. Now I see myself,
trussed tight in love, the blanket drawn around my chin.
My hair in curling rags, the patient efforts of a mother
so determined, like her friends, to recreate
the Shirley Temple darlings of these times.
I wince in retrospect. Barbaric custom, winding
such intransigent lank tresses in white strips of rag.
Another form of bandaging? Repair of subtler forms
of faults, inadequacies, less notable than bleeding knees?
The miserable nights, with aching head and stabbing pain
each turn when sausage curls catch on the pillow slip.
Then stinging eyes when it's time for removal, and impatient words.
'Don't be a baby now. You're six years old. Too big to cry
at something that's so little. And think how beautiful you'll look.'
Vain hope indeed. A mousy child, which even corkscrewed curls
and mother's partiality could scarce disguise.
I turn in bed, and feel again the tautness of the bindings.
They tug my scalp and bring tears to my eyes.
An early lesson in the female search for beauty, and the sacrifices
that we make. A pattern set, adhered to down the years,
in spite of recognition that it isn't worth the effort.
But compensation as I lie there, for on the wall
the morning peaches come; my child's heart sings
to see them hanging full of promise.
I watch in fascination though aware – yes, even then –
with prescience their promise is illusion, like themselves.

Claire, 2009/Clara, 1944

The room's my haven; it's security. At eight,
the pictures on the wall are comforting. For many years
I do not think to question why, when Jesus, so serene, raised arms
to bless the flock of children gathered round his feet,
in all those blue-eyed, blonde-haired children, there is
only one dark face. And he a loincloth wearer...
The word 'inclusive' has not reached my ears.

It is an Anglo world, a wartime world,
and foreigners are those in other places, strange and distant,
where our brave soldiers go to fight. Or Faye next door,
whose boyfriend Bill sends cards and photographs,
which she, a teenage giggling girl, shows off to me.
'Bill's with the fuzzy wuzzies' so she tells me.
This is the way I learn my world – strange lands far north,
where dark-skinned people with huge mops of hair,
stand beaming next to grinning slouch-hat boys,
while mates take photos for the girls back home.
'New Guinea,' Faye says doubtfully, uncertain as the child
she speaks to, just exactly where that is.
For war is trenches in the local park, inadequate protection
for when predicted bombs might fall. (They never came.)
Or ration cards, and savings stamps at school.
'Our effort for the brave boys at the front,' Miss Martin says.
There came a day her eyes were reddened, and the other teachers
spoke in hushed tones of how we had to make a special effort
to be good for her. 'What's a fiancé, Mum?' I asked that night,
'And how do they get lost?'

Then suddenly it's ended, in a blaze of dancing in the streets
and city jubilation. My father's newspaper, the evening ritual,
brought home like clockwork every night,
just slightly crumpled from train trip contortions,
now with its blazoned headlines – almost the whole page.
VP. It's Victory Day in the Pacific. A vivid red and black,
and pictures of rejoicing crowds with waving flags.

But little alters in my bedroom in those years;
my world at home has always been secure.

Clara, Blues Interlude 1

Girls' faces turn towards me.
In the playground a sea of hostile faces turns towards me.
These are the schoolyard blues.

They swing towards me with intensity.
The bodies mass, increase in density.
The voices rise to a crescendo.
I shut my ears – diminuendo –
But nothing that I do obliterates
the ringleader, the one who hates
me and creates each day
a time of torment they call play.

My name sounds German.
It gives away my background, because my name sounds German.
These are the post-war schoolyard blues.

For some the looks are only curious.
But many faces redden – furious –
for they've lost uncles, fathers, brothers.
And all have heard at least of others
dead at the enemy German hands.
Now right before them one child stands
to bear their anger at the race.
So here I wait with tear-stained face…

The teacher comes to see what's happening.
The mercy-bringing teacher strolls to see what's happening in the yard.
Soon for today the schoolyard blues will end.

Clara, 1945

'Don't mind them, pet,' my father's voice is kind.
'People will forget.'
He's learned his patience a hard way.
Jobs lost: 'Can't have you workin' here.
I'm sorry, Joe, but lots of customers won't buy
from chaps who have a German name.
I know you're Aussie as the rest of us,
but they don't see that, so you unnerstand
I gotta let you go.'

No matter that he's tried so hard
to recreate himself as just another ordinary chap.
Most times he talks like all the other dads I know.
Though sometimes, when he's with my aunties,
I listen to him speak – it doesn't seem
like Dad at all. He almost sounds
a foreigner. But then he comes back home
with Mum and Paul and me and he's my dad again.

I hear my parents talking in the night –
their room is opposite; the muttered sounds
of conversation drift across the hall.
Language adults talk, discussing things
not for their children's ears. 'Should we change
our name? Lots of others have.'
'I just dunno, luv. If we did, me dad'd turn,
I tell you, in his grave. Proud of his name
and of the background too. I'm not too keen.'
I listen, trying hard to understand.
Yet in our climate of the post-war attitudes,
and lingering hostility, it makes good sense.

For now he takes a labourer's job and practises
the patience that he preaches. Uses night-time hours
to keep alive the skills that are denied the chance
for daytime usage. But scars are left,
and he will never lose the need to know
his job's secure, and that he can provide
for all his family's needs. For this is why
he's left behind the little country town,
the old familiar networks he has always known.
'You kids will have the chances that I didn't.
You'll get the schooling I missed out on.'
He watches us with pride as year by year,
spurred by his interest, we intensify our efforts
and bring home the prizes that he values so.

Claire, February 1951

Our dinner times are placid. Little comes
to ruffle daily trivia. Small things suffice
for conversation. The shocking price of butter;
just how the coupons aren't enough
to get a decent piece of meat.
'These sausages are tasty, though –
Don't you think so? I made an onion sauce
that Lizzie found in last week's *Woman's Day*.'
She's anxious for response, lest good advice
from her next door has been a blunder…
He chews on stolidly, and nods.
'Yeah, they're real good. I always like a snag.'
The meal resumes its silence.
'I tell you, luv,' he says, fork held aloft,
'You ought to see the sausages those DPs eat –
the stuff they bring for lunch some days!
Cripes! The smell's enough to knock a bloke
for six! I dunno how they eat it.'
The meal resumes its silence.
Paul looks up hesitant. 'What's that mean, Dad?
What's a DP?' He's only nine, but I – fifteen –
am equally unsure. And even Mum's look
shows her uncertainty.
'The Balts,' he answers, masticating. 'Reffos, kids.
The ones who've come here since the war.'
He sees that still we haven't understood.
The world of politics, just like arts and music,
rarely impinges on our safe suburban lives,
and international affairs are way beyond our ken.
He tries to tell us what he's learned.

'The war…' he starts. We nod. We know the war.
'Well, when it ended, lots of them had nowhere
left to live. And then the commies came
and they took over lots of places, so the people
who lived there just couldn't stay.'
'Why not?' I ask. They've said at school
that I'm a bright child, always eager to learn more.
But now Dad's caught; his eyes grow vague.
'The commies took it over – took their land
and if they had a lot of money took that too.
So lots of them just upped and left. And sometimes
they say it was hard. Almost like…
escaping.' Our eyes grow round. We know
about escape. A steady diet of war films
and Biggles as our staple hero's taught us well
about escapes. But I'm still curious:
'What was that word you called them, Dad? D what?'
This he knows, and so he's quick to answer.
'DPs – it stands for what they are, pet – they're
displaced – D for displaced and P for persons. It means
they don't have homes or countries any more.
And that's why they come here. We bring them
to Australia, so they can start again.'

Claire, February 1951

I lie in bed that night and wonder.
Just what would it be like?
To have to leave your home, your friends,
even your books and toys behind,
and find another place to live,
another country?
What if you couldn't speak the language?
How would people understand you?

The shadows on my bedroom wall
are flickering with passing cars
along the rain-slicked street outside.
The sound is comforting, but still
I shiver, and reach up to pull the blind
that final inch, enclosing this
my world, which I now keep secure.

Claire, Friday 23 March 1951

Another night, another dinner.
'It's fish and chips tonight.' It must have been a Friday.
'We're not RC!' I hear how Mum explains it carefully
to Liz next door. 'But Joe he really likes
his fish and chips on Friday night.'

It's Paul again who asks, 'Tell us some more
about the DPs, Dad.'

'Well, when they come here on the ships, they have
to find them work to do. So first of all they send them
to a place to stay. Somewhere up north. Might even be
in New South Wales.' We look impressed.
Our Melbourne-oriented minds find this
another world. Across the border! Alien soil, indeed.
'Yeah, Bonegilla. That's the name.'
We try it tentatively. Hard to say.
'So first they stay there till they find them jobs.
The government, y'know.' He gestures vaguely.
'They have to find them work to do.
That's why we bring them here. They need a place to live,
and we need workers. We can always use them
on the railways.' That's where Dad works, we know.
'We're always needing more men than we've got.
And they're good workers too. Nice blokes, they are,
that's when you get to know them. Chap with me now –
name's Viktor…but they call him Vic.' Paul giggles.
So do I. Viktor is a name we know from comic books,
a super hero's name. Dad frowns, and so we stop.

He's not amused. 'Good worker, Viktor. Doesn't mind
getting his hands dirty, though it's not the sort of work
that he's been used to. White-collar jobs
he used to have, that's pretty clear. I had to teach him
everything from scratch. But he's a mate.'

'Any more chips?' asks Mum. 'Well then, you help me clear
the table, Claire, and I'll get pudding.'
'What is it?' asks Paul eagerly. 'You wait and see!'
She smiles, relents. 'Your favourite, Paulie, chocolate pud
and chocolate sauce.' But Dad is ruminating.
'Tough on Viktor. He won't get food like this,
living where he does. He could do with feeding up –
a bit of your home cooking would be a treat for him.'

'I s'pose,' she offers doubtfully, 'we could invite
him here some time. Where does he live?'
'A hostel somewhere. It's just men. I think.
From what he says the woman running it is pretty tough.'

'Well then, you ask him, Joe. Maybe a Sunday dinner.
I could do a roast.'

Claire, Sunday 1 April 1951

It's quite exciting, really. We don't have many visitors.
And Mum has ordered cream to have with Sunday dinner.
That's a treat. The milkman's left it with the bottles
on the front veranda. I get to wear my best dress
and to keep it on, even after we get home from church.
My hair is in two plaits, with big bows at the bottom.
Now that I'm a high school girl the painful days
of manufactured curls are over, and the long white strips of rag
are finished. Not out in garbage bins, of course.
Our way of life is frugal – nothing's wasted. I rather think
they may have found a new life tying up the climbing beans
in Daddy's vegie garden. Between the vegies and the chooks
we're almost self-sustaining in suburbia. Shades
of my father's country past.

Dad's gone to meet him at the station. 'He'll come by train –
no problems there. But then you never know,
he might get lost in following the map I've drawn for him
to get him to our place. No, you two can wait here
and keep your mother company.'

She's oddly nervous. 'Where did you say that he was from?'
she's asked last night at dinner. It's a new name for us too.
'Czechoslovakia,' says Dad. Another one for us
to try experimentally. 'How can we talk to him?'
Paul has asked. 'And can he talk to us?'
Dad smiles benignly. 'Yeah, he's quite an educated cove.
His English isn't bad at all. I think he speaks
some other lingos too.' Mum looks relieved.

We wait excitedly beside the gate, then Paul climbs
up the fence. 'They're coming now.' We run inside
to tell her, as we've been instructed. She smooths her hair,
takes off the apron. She's wearing her good dress.
The dining table's laid. The best white cloth, well blued
and almost crackly stiff with starch, and serviettes
and flowers in a vase. No kitchen table eating, this.

Claire, Sunday 1 April 1951

I'm not sure quite what we had pictured. Someone like a being
from another planet, maybe. Almost an anticlimax, this.
He's just a small dark man, with finely chiselled face
and dark eyes, thoughtful as he greets us.
He takes my mother's hand, half raises it towards his lips
and lowers his head – then thinks again, contents himself
with a long handshake. 'This is indeed a pleasure, madam.'
We kids suppress a snigger. 'Madam' to our mum.

Then it's our turn. 'Your son?' He looks at Paul,
surprises him by holding out his hand, which Paul,
unused to such attention, shakes but looks embarrassed.
'*Dobry den*,' he says, quite serious. 'This is our hello.'
He turns to me: 'And you are Clara?' I shoot
a furious look at Dad. Is this what he has called me
at his work? 'She's usually known as Claire
at school,' Mum hastens to put in, alerted by
the look of fury on my face. I've worked so hard
at fitting in, and Clara doesn't sit well with the Pamelas and Joans.

And yet, surprisingly, when I hear 'Clara' on his lips
it doesn't sound so bad.

'So say hello to Mr Kasals, you kids.' We chorus dutifully.
We've been well drilled.

He's carrying something. Now he hands a small box
to my mother. 'I bring the chocolates for you.'
Flustered, she takes them with some murmured thanks.
But Paul and I cast quick appreciative glances
at each other. A treat we haven't seen for a long time.

Doss, Sunday 1 April 1951

I really didn't quite know what to think
when Joe invited him; I wasn't sure
just what a foreigner would eat or drink.
But then when he came in through the front door
I knew I didn't need to fuss too much
about how he would see us, really rather
how he would feel at always being such
a stranger – almost being like the other
in houses that were different from his home
with people speaking languages that he
might feel made him seem more alone –
much more perhaps than we would ever see.

His manners are just lovely – as I said
to Lizzie next door later on that day.
'It's almost like a book that I once read –
these chaps from overseas sure have a way
of making you feel like a queen.
I'll swear he almost kissed my hand.
Mind you, I don't know how I would have been
if he had done it.' Don't think she'd understand
exactly how I felt. In fact, the way she eyed
me off, I nearly blushed. But then I don't think she
has ever read a book – and after all she can't abide
the reffos in the weekend papers – stories we
talked about last Monday. Well, I suppose
until you meet them you don't really know
that though they come from far off lands those
people really are like us, and not so
strange. 'Well, Doss,' she said next day to me,
'It takes all sorts to make a world, I guess.

I wonder if you'll have him here again.' Then she
went back through the fence gate to her own busyness.
And I went on with mine; it's Monday washing day
and with Joe's overalls and the two kids' stuff –
I'll swear I can't imagine what they play –
so when I've finished I'll have had enough.

Doss, Monday afternoon, 2 April 1951

I was getting clothes in from the line
and thinking as I tugged at one stuck peg
I wonder what it's like, so fine
a gentleman to almost have to beg
another land to take him in, and then
to have to leave his home and friends
and never really be sure when
or in fact how the whole thing ends.

I'd asked him what about his wife, for Joe
had told me that he thought he had a wife.
'I am not able yet to bring her here, and so
she stays in camps.' 'But that's no life
for either of you,' Joe was quick to say.
He answered fast: 'Men must work, so wives must go
to other camps. Mildura is quite far away
but families must go there. There are many so.'
Joe's always been kind-hearted, has my man.
Talking about it almost spoiled the day –
I really wish that we could help them find some plan.
But asking questions always is Claire's way.
'Why didn't she come with you?' Mr K looked sad,
and so did Paul. Claire likes to get things clear,
but Paulie's more soft-hearted like his dad.
For Claire it's simple: why not bring her here?
'There is no place where she can live,' he said.
'Where I live only menfolk are permitted.
It was in documents that we were read
when first I went there: Only men admitted.'

'It's called a hostel, luv,' Joe said to me.
'Most of the DPs have to live in these.
To find another room today just has to be
almost impossible. Not a case of please
or thank you – there's nothing round to rent
and landlords pick and choose who gets a place.
It hardly matters how much money's spent,
you're simply told there isn't living space!'

I would have liked to ask him how she felt
but something told me better not to say
more on the topic. We had dealt
with misery enough to cope with for today.
The kids were good; they quite took to the chap
and he was friendly, talked to them as though
they were grown up. At last I said I'd wrap
some food up for him when he had to go.
He looked quite touched, and said it was real kind.
That sort of gratitude makes things worthwhile.
I figure that you never really mind
making an effort if it gets a thanks and smile.

Doss, Tuesday 3 April 1951

I said to Joe last night, as we got into bed,
'Did Mr Kasals talk at all about
the visit?' 'Not too much,' Joe said,
'but then he's not the sort to shout
his business for the world to hear.
Said he enjoyed the day, thanked you for food.
I reckon where he lives it's pretty clear
that what she serves up isn't all that good,
so eating your beaut tucker was a treat.
He did say that he had received a letter
from his missus, and he looked real beat.
Don't think it made him feel much better.
She hates it where she is. The camp
is awful. Little tin huts that they've got them in –
stinking hot in summer; now it's damp
and cold with winter coming on. Reckon it's a sin,'
said Joe, 'to keep them living separate.
I know how I'd be feeling if they told
us we had to live like that, for months apart.
At night in bed it must be bloody cold.'
'Don't swear, Joe!' I said automatic-like.
But I could see his point real well.
If I weren't trying to be ladylike
I could have said myself, it must be hell.

Joe, Thursday 5 April 1951

Funny watching Viktor
at our house. Not really
the same coot that I see
everyday. There in the sheds
he's quiet, hardly has a word
to say. Just listens
when we show him what to do.
He's quick – I'll hand him that.
We had to teach him
everything. First day Jim spat.
'Don't think he knows
a spanner from a wrench,'
he said. 'He won't last long.'
But then Jim had to eat his words.
It's six weeks, and he's stayed.
First time he put on overalls
it almost made us laugh.
Sort of like fancy dress –
just didn't seem quite right
on him. But then he settled in
real fast, and soon
the other blokes forgot that
he's so different.

Odd seeing him at home, though.
Doss had made everything
real nice. I saw she was
impressed. He has a way
of being posh, but not
so that you'd take offence.
I like him. He's not
one of us – but he's a mate.

Joe, Friday 6 April 1951

Once read a book –
was one of Doss's –
funny title
Grapes of Wrath.
Only other time I'd heard
that strange word 'wrath'
was somewhere in the Bible.
Not sure why he called
the book by such a name.
But something in it stuck.
Early on,
there's this cove
coming out of prison.
He's on the tramp
and aiming to get home.
A truckie picks him up
and asks him how he's doing.
This chap – name's Tom, I think –
says, 'I just keep on going.
Put one foot after the other.'
I'm not a reader, but
that stuck.
About all we can do.
One foot, and then the other.
That's what life's about.
S'pose that's what
Viktor's doing. Just putting
down one foot, and then the other.

Joe, Sunday 8 April 1951

Working in
the vegie garden.
I was digging
spuds. Doss in
the next bed,
weeding carrots.
I stopped a minute
for a breather.
Looked at her,
face reddened
as she stooped
and gathered up
the box of weeds.
Felt something
warm inside me.
Thought of
Viktor, on his own.
'What say we stop, love,
have a cup of tea?'

Joe, Tuesday 10 April 1951

Can't get it
out of my head.
It's just not right.
Viktor on his own.
That woman
sitting there
in Bonegilla,
or Mildura,
or wherever,
mis'rable
as sin. That's what
it is – a sin.
I sat in church
last Sunday
and I thought,
'Joe, it's just not
right. This isn't
what the good book
says. We're meant
to love our neighbours
as ourselves.
There's got to be
some way that we can help.
There's no flats
to be had.
They queue up
waiting at each ad.
And when a landlady
puts up a window sign
they come from
miles around.
A bloke like Viktor
doesn't have a show.

Joe, Wednesday 11 April 1951

Put it to Doss last night
in bed. Best place
to have a yack.
I said to her,
'Don't want this
talked about to kids
until we work out
what to do.'
'You're right,' she said.
'They always say that
little pitchers…'
Not sure what she meant.
But anyways, as soon
as I said what
was on my mind,
she was right with me.
Knew she'd feel the same.

She's practical, my Doss.
She worked it out.
She didn't want to put
the two kids in one room.
'Can't do that any more.
Claire's just too old.'
Still find it hard to call her
Claire. She's Clara,
far as I'm concerned.
My mum's name, after all…
But I could see the point
that Doss was making.
The girl's fifteen.

Won't be long now
before she's grown up,
thinking about boys.
But Doss was planning things.
'This won't be for long.
What say we put her
in with me? Then you
and Paul can have
the dining room…
We can shift furniture
around to make it work.
The dining table might
just fit in with the
lounge suite. Then those
two can have for their own use
the other front room.'

I mulled it over.

'We'll have to charge them
something. After all,
he's got his pride.'

'With what food costs,
these days,' Doss said,
'no way that we can keep them
as a charity. We're not the Salvos,
that's for sure! A bit of extra cash
will come in handy.'

But then we both agreed
we'd keep it small.

It's not a great
arrangement, I'll admit.
But if we do it, Viktor
can bring down his missus.
They can stay with us
until they find another place.

Viktor, Thursday 12 April 1951

This man…these people…hard to understand.
I work beside these men each day, and wonder.
They seem to me, an outsider, another race.
They laugh among themselves – to each other
friendly. What is the word they have?
They're mates. That is their word for it.
I do not understand their jokes.
They are like children. Like a schoolyard,
they play tricks upon each other,
and they laugh. But somehow good to see.
At me they look uneasily. I am the stranger
in their midst. The foreigner. At first
they did not think that I could talk to them
or know what they were saying.
Then realised. 'He knows the lingo' –
It was Joe who told them. Now sometimes
they look at me to see what I might think,
but never ask. 'He knows the lingo…'
Now I learn this word. The lingo.
I wonder just how it might seem to them
if they were told how many of these 'lingos'
are familiar to me. The Greek and Latin
of my childhood schooling, drilled by tutors,
checked by my father's careful eye;
the French we spoke at home, and German,
English, some Hungarian, a little Russian –
all these familiar, needed in my dealings
with clients from so many lands. Oh yes,
my friends – you who are not my friends –
I speak your lingo, and so many more.

It's only Joe who talks to me.
A different man. And yet he's one of them.
He has the same simplicity. But kindly.
He tries to be my friend
and in a place where I am friendless
this is good.

I try now to remember how it was.
The men who worked for me – what were they?
The days when I was like the one these call the Boss.
The years when I walked through the rows
and men and women at machines looked
anxiously at me to see if I was pleased.
The time when I could say to this one
'Come' and that one 'Go' and make a young boy
smile because I nodded at his work.

All gone. The labour of my years in other hands.
So what is left for me?
Another land? New life? To start again?

Strange now to be among these men
who laugh together, and are friends.
But look at me uneasily. I am the foreigner.

Viktor, Friday 13 April 1951

He asked me to his home, and somehow
there I knew that this was strange for them
just as it was for me.
The foreigner – and in their home. I could see
that they had tried so hard to make me welcome.
I tried to put aside the memories of home, of nights
with gleaming silver and fine glassware,
with music playing and the wit and laughter
of like minds round a dinner table.
Instead I looked at Joe, his cheerful smile,
the woman red-faced from her efforts in the kitchen,
two children shy, uneasy with this unaccustomed guest.
But anxious, all, to make me feel at home.

These are good people, and I smiled
to find myself there in that house at peace.

So now another weekend comes, to sit alone,
and think of her, Irena, wonder
what she does, alone there in the camp.
This is no life.
What have we done, in coming here?

Viktor, Sunday night, 15 April 1951

Irena.
Nights are worst. Nights when I feel
again the silken ripple of your skin
moving underneath my seeking hands.
Your body quiver at my touch. Your breathing
shallow, quickening as your passion mounts.
The way you lie, eyes closed, demure,
until with calculated practised ease,
you part your legs when you are ready for me.
The nights when you are willing…
Too many when you turn away, pretend
you are asleep. A lie we both are suited by.
I suffer your rejections with more ease
when we can cover it with such pretences.

Now in this barren time without you, I have trained
at least my body to accept the separations
you have long taught me.

I watch the others go. 'Come, Viktor,
there are many women in this place.
We show you where we go.' I shake my head.
'The price is little. Come with us.'
I never yet have had to pay for women.
No, not in coinage. Perhaps I too have paid
in other ways. Your cost is high, and it may be
the price is more than I should choose to give.
Men in this house, this hostel as they call it,
men have their needs – until their women come
they can find ways of meeting them.
But mine are different. Yours is the body
that I need. But nights are worst.
The nights, Irena.

Viktor, Monday 16 April 1951

I do not understand them.
These people. They are different.

Joe comes to me this morning, says he wants
to 'have a yack'. Sees that I do not understand.
'A talk,' he says. 'I want to ask you something.'

I wait, a little fearful. What could this man
be asking of me? There is nothing I can give him.

We sit together, and he coughs. 'Been thinking…'
That is how he starts.

Still now, though hours have passed, I do not
fully understand. They want, he tells me,
to offer us a place within their home.
How can they do this thing?
The house is small.
But he makes earnest explanations.
'We've worked it out,' he tells me
almost shyly. 'We'll double up in bedrooms
while you're there. You and your missus
can sleep in Clara's room, and we can shift around.
Won't be forever, after all. Some day you'll find
a place somewhere. And in between
you'll have a home with us. So you can be
together with your wife.'

I find it hard to speak. What he is offering
is almost more than I can comprehend.
He sees I have no words, and looks away.
'You'd do the same, I know,' he says.
'It's what mates do. They help each other out.'
I shake my head. He is not right, of course.
My friends are not like this. We drink,
we talk, we laugh together, yes. But this!
No, this is not our way. They would not
do this for me. And I would not for them.

His act is like a gift. And, like a gift,
must be received with gratitude.
My heart lifts at the thought. To stop
Irena's tears of misery, and tell her
she can leave the camp, and come to me.
I nod acceptance, but I cannot speak.
There are no words to tell him what I feel.
The goodness of this simple man is grace
that leaves me humbled.
I say only to him, *'Dekuji.'*
This is a thank you from my heart.

Viktor, Tuesday 17 April 1951

I telephone. Not easy from this place.
The little box stands in a cupboard
underneath the stairs. The landlady suspicious.
'It's interstate, y'know, and Mister K – '
She finds our names so hard to say, that this
is how she names us all, as Mister K and Mister Z
and Mister T – we are her alphabet of lodgers –
'Long-distance calls cost money, Mister K.'

So much the time it takes, there at the other place.
They have to go and seek Irena. I can feel
her running, anxious, from the little room,
that space inside the Nissen hut that was our home
the weeks we waited to find what would happen next.
I should have thought ahead to her alarm,
fearful what a call from Melbourne means.
I should have told them, 'Do not let her be concerned;
tell her that there is nothing wrong. Tell her
good news.' Care is needed with Irena.
So many years together – still I do not think!

But then, to say to her, that she can leave
the place, that barren outpost of the world
they call Mildura! Leave the miserable hut
where nights on nights she sobs herself to sleep,
where she has clung to me and begged
that we might get away from heat and flies
and wretchedness and lack of company.

She weeps with joy, and laughs through tears.
We talk (the woman at the stairs with clock in hand
times every moment) – then I bring back to mind
what we have said. 'In English, *mílácku.*
This is our land now. We must speak in English.'
The woman with the clock nods her approval,
and even gives a grudging smile at news
that I have found somewhere to bring my wife –
then tells me how much I must pay her when I leave.

Doss, Thursday 19 April 1951

I really want to make it nice so that
she'll feel at home. I know the place she's at
has been a misery. He told us how
the food they're served there now
is hardly fit to eat. Not to their taste
at all! He says they hate to waste
what's put before them, but to eat
it is impossible. Joe says it's hard to beat
my cooking, so I really want to make
this time with us a good time for her sake.
As well, I've really done my level best
to make their room a cosy little nest.
I've moved Claire in with me, and all her things –
my goodness me! The stuff that girl brings
has me throwing up my hands
in horror. Don't think she understands
how hard this new arrangement is for me
as well as her. But then we have to be
a bit compassionate, says Joe.
He's right. I feel that too, and so
I'm more than willing to put myself out
although I sometimes feel a sneaking doubt
that this will work as well as those two men
seem to expect. I hope she's nice, 'cos then
it could be good to have another woman here.
The kids are kids, and Joe's a dear
but I'd be happy to make a new friend –
that made me willing to go out and spend
a bit on setting up their room, and make it nice.
Mind you, I didn't quite expect the price
I'd have to pay for that new spread.

But then, the one that Claire had on her bed
was really getting old and worn.
Next I saw the curtains, slightly torn
and mended. Neatly, mind, but then that too
made me uneasy. So I've gone and bought some new
ones. I guess the extra bit of cash in hand
they'll pay, will cover it, and Joe will understand.
He looked the whole room over and he gave a smile.
'I think they should be happy here a while.'

Claire, Friday 20 April 1951

It's tomorrow that they come. The house
has been so changed it's topsy-turvy, as Mum says.
I'm not sure how I feel about it.
It's exciting, that's for sure. A bit romantic, really.
Like star-crossed lovers, kept apart by fate,
and now we're helping them to be together.
Except they're old, of course. I don't think
you count as star-crossed lovers at that age.
He must be forty – but there's something
makes you feel he's not that old. Sort of
Rhett Butler, in a way. I could almost see him
leaning over her, and saying, as Rhett did,
'My dear, I just don't give a damn.'
We practised it at school, that line, one lunchtime
in the cloakroom. We tried to guess how it would feel
if someone looked at you that way. Giggled,
but shivered too.

It's got its other side. I'm bunking in with Mum,
and Paul's with Dad. He doesn't mind, but me,
I'm not so sure. I couldn't share with Paul,
that's true. I wouldn't want to anyway.
But then Mum's old, and getting fat,
and takes forever putting hair in curlers every night.
I miss my room; it was my place.
I even had to take my pictures off the walls.
I packed away my ornaments and almost cried,
but Mum was quite determined that they had to go.

I wonder what she'll be like, Mrs Viktor –
he said that we're to call him Viktor. When we do as
Dad had told us, call him Mr Kasals, then he feels
too old. So even Paul's supposed to call him Viktor.
I guess then that we'll say Irena for her.
It's such a lovely name. It sounds all gliding, somehow.
Irena means 'peaceful' – I read that in a book.
I told him – Viktor – and he laughed. But
not the way you laugh at something funny.

Joe, Sunday 22 April 1951

Must admit
I was a bit surprised
just how much stuff
they brought with them.
Guess they had some way
of getting it out here.
I've stacked the boxes
in the shed.
It took a while
to move my tools
and make some room.

'These things we bring
from home,' she said.
He smiled,
apologetic-like,
and shrugged.
'You know how women are…'
I scratched my head.

Saw how Doss looked at her
and quickly took her pinny off.
She'd worn her best dress
just in case.
Reckon she was glad.
Bit of a fashion plate,
Irena. Blondie too.
Used to be on stage
so Viktor told me.

Bit too much make-up
for my liking.
I like a woman
to look natural.
Not so tarted up.

Claire couldn't take
her eyes off her.

Doss, Monday 23 April 1951

I'd made some lamingtons for after tea,
that special recipe from Lizzie, and I must say he
seemed to enjoy them, but I don't quite know
about her – she's a picky so-and-so,
who fiddled round and nibbled at the chook
I'd made for them. One of our own. I only cook
a bird of ours at times when I do feel
it's worth the sacrifice of eggs. It was a meal
I felt quite proud of, and I'd have to say
that Joe and Viktor thanked me in a way
that made me feel it was worthwhile.
She didn't say a word, or even smile.
She might just be real tired, and it's true
that moving's a real cow. I know that you
can sometimes just be tuckered out –
too flat to even talk, and there's no doubt
they had a lot of stuff to shift. Really quite
a bit more than I'd thought. It was a sight
to see the front veranda under such a pile
of boxes. It sure took a while
and lots of help to get them all inside.
No wonder when they finished that she cried –
although he took great pains to make it very clear
that they were both real grateful to be here.

Viktor, Tuesday 24 April 1951

Irena, *Liebchen, chérie, láska,* it will be better soon.
We will leave here. This is not life forever.
These people and this house, this room,
this is another stop along our way.
Remember, at the least, here we can be
together. That is worth so much.
And they are kindly people. I understand
that this must seem to you so strange,
this house so small, our room – I know
this is not what we had.
But think, Irena, all those months that you have waited
enduring life in Bonegilla. Then the other place.
Surely these were worse.
Think further back. The ship.
And then before that, camps. The roads,
the packing up our home to leave
before the Russians came, the sacrifice
of so much, all the things we loved that we have left,
so little we could bring. Our lives
packed in these boxes. We have endured all this
in promise of a better life to come.

This room is little, yes. These people strange,
their way is not our way. But it is home for us
this little time. So cease the weeping,
think instead that here we can at last find peace
together. Turn to me tonight, Irena,
not away.

Irena, Wednesday 25 April 1951

Three days. I shall be mad. I walk the room.
I hear her at this door.
'A cup of tea?'
'I drink it not.'
'Coffee then, love?'
She call me 'love'!
I stay in room. I will not sit with her. I cry.

I must make effort, Viktor say.
The room is ugly. Walls a colour make me ill.
Bright colours on this cover on the bed –
they hurt the eyes. I shut them while I walk
the door to window, back again.

Viktor have not tell me
he go each day from here while still is dark.
And near to dark when he and Joe return each night.
The days are long. I shall be mad.

Irena, Thursday 26 April 1951

I dream last night of camp. Still it is
nightmare for me. We all like animals –
like cattle in big pen. Like at my father's,
but here we animals, not allowed in house.
We eat in common room, big tables,
with people not known to us. We sleep
in small place – only curtain make us
private – separate from other family. Their child –
it cry for half the night. Day follow day.
We wait for man to tell us where we go.
I beg to Viktor. Please, America. There
I find work as actor. I will be star
in movie. I have meet in Praha man who is
director. He has tell me, you come Hollywood.
I make you big big star in film.
I willing even learn the English –
ugly – not like Français, even Deutsch –
if it make me the star.
But Viktor say too many want America.
For this we wait here many years.
Shorter wait if choose another land.
So where? I say him. Where you wish? He ask.
I care not. He ask again, 'Australia?'
It matter not. I wish America, and be movie star.
But anywhere, to get away from here.
When I wake from dream, I still in
nightmare. This land is also nightmare.

Doss, Friday 27 April 1951

Lizzie, I tell you I can't make this work.
You know me; I'm not one to shirk
my duty, but I just don't know
how I can ever make a go
of this arrangement. She won't talk
and when I asked her if she'd like to walk
down to the shops with me, you should have seen
the look she gave me, like a queen
staring at a peasant. Made me feel so small –
I don't think this is going to work at all.
I tell you straight; if not for you next door
I don't think I'd put up with any more!

Viktor, Sunday 29 April 1951

Dear heart, now it is time for change. I have waited
for one week, for time to bring you to new mind.
Now it is time to speak. We cannot live like this.
You cannot live like this.

So much you wanted to leave Bonegilla and the camps.
These people have been kind, have made it possible.
We cannot treat them so. The woman, she is hurt.
The man, he does not understand.
The children – they sit at the dinner in the nights
and look at you. They wonder what is wrong.
And I? I grow despairing. What more can I do?

Irena, you are actress. You can play a role.
Be the grateful guest within this house.
Befriend the woman. Charm them all
the way you charmed all those who knew us
in the old life. It is another part
for you to play – and you can do this well.
This is your greatest role – show us what you can be.
So I shall ring the curtain up for you.

Doss, Thursday 3 May 1951

You'd hardly credit how she's changed.
You'd almost think that we'd arranged
a swap for someone else. She looks
at me, shows me her fashion books
and tries to talk to me the way I thought
a guest who's staying here should do. I ought
to be a bit suspicious, I suppose –
a change like this as anybody knows
is not to be relied on. Then again
perhaps she's realised that when
you're stuck somewhere, it's up to you
to make a go of it. Well, that's what I'd do!

Joe, Friday 4 May 1951

You know what kids
are like – always full of
questions. Viktor had been
helping Paul with planes.
When Doss gave us a hoy
and called us to the table
Paul got his back up –
didn't want to stop
what they were doing.
'Your mother calls us,'
Viktor said – quite firm.
But Paul kept at him
all through dinner.
'Can we finish it tonight?'
Got to admire the chap.
He's really patient
with the lad. He smiled
and nodded. 'Viktor
knows so much!' Paul's
real impressed. 'How come
you know so much about
these planes?' For a minute
I had a feeling that it was
a question Viktor didn't like.
Then he laid down his knife
and fork, and looked at Irena.
She stared at him, and
shrugged her shoulders.

'My younger brother,
Jaroslav, he went to England
and flew Lancasters. Many
Czech boys did this in the war.'
Our lad was real impressed.
'Wow! What's he doing now?
For a minute Viktor went on
eating. Chewing sort of slow.
'He was shot down in Germany.'
Even Paul shut up.
'More spuds?' I asked Viktor.
He shook his head.
'But I enjoy your dinner, Doss.
I thank you – it is always good.'

Viktor, Friday 4 May 1951

Still now, Irena, when I think on Jaroslav,
I can remember well that last night
that we were together. He was so young.
A boy only. He should have been at school.
At university. A student. He should have had
my youth. At school is still where I can see him,
an eager boy, so young, until the Germans came…
The closing of St Johannes Gymnasium,
the end of childhood for him. He told me
of the work they put the boys to do,
the clean up duties after bomb attacks, the building
of the rail tracks in the Pilsen works.
'This is no work for Czechs,' he said. And looked
at me with scorn. 'How can you do it? You make boots
for German troops. You help the enemy!'
I kept my temper. 'It is this or lose the factories.'
'You and our father bring dishonour to our family!'
When one is young, talk of honour is important.
'You tell your wife to dance with German officers
in nightclubs. She has told me this.' The young
are quick to judge. 'There are things you do not know.'
This was all I could say to him. It would not
have been wise to tell the boy the way we used
the warehouse for resistance meetings, or how
the German favour worked to help our cause.
Even you did not know this, Irena, for women
cannot keep still tongues. But hard to have you
look your scorn at me, especially when we found
that Jaroslav had gone to England. The letter
that he left. 'Someone must keep our family
name and honour. I go to join the Czech Free Force.'

You blame me for his death, I know it.
And I? I can remember too the way he looked at you.
The way his face would redden when you smiled
and touched his hand. You think I did not see
the way he felt for you? You think I did not know
that you were flattered by a young boy's adoration?
He went to England not just for the honour
of our family – but to win your smile.

Claire, Saturday 5 May 1951

She's really beautiful, Irena is. Just like a movie star.
Viktor says that once upon a time she used to be on stage.
An actress. Really! But not in proper movies –
in stage plays, he was saying. I said I'd never seen
a play on stage – just read them in the books
we're studying at school. He looked surprised,
and said they'd have to see if something
could be done about that. They do these things –
I guess it's being European. This afternoon
he took her to a gallery to look at paintings, now tonight
they've gone to see a film. Something on in town.
It had a foreign name. It's on at that new movie place
for foreign films they've got in Russell Street.
Miss Rodney said we ought to go to see
these films, not just the local flicks. She's travelled overseas.
She has ideas quite different from the other teachers
even though she's old. We think she must be almost forty.
Mum sniffed when Viktor said that they'd be out that night.
'Well, don't forget the last train home's at ten.'
But afterwards I heard her say to Dad,
'Not good enough, I s'pose. The local pictures
aren't enough for them. I've heard about
these foreign films, and all the things they get up to
in them.' 'Oh well,' Dad said, 'nice for them
to hear the people speak in their own language,
and not in English all the time. They must get tired,
always having to speak words that they weren't
brought up with.' I hear them in the night –
the bedroom walls are thin – the bedroom that was mine –
and in that room they talk away sometimes real fast.

It sounds quite strange. They're talking more now.
She's not crying quite so much. It made me sad
to hear her all last week, and even though
she hardly looks at me, I watch her all the time.

Irena, Saturday 5 May 1951

I say him, 'No! Not here. Not in this house.'
This he must see. This room. So small,
unangenehm! Impossible.
The walls, so thin. Here every little sound
will be through all the house.

'So long,' he try to tell me.
'I need you,' he say to me.
'All these weeks alone.'

He has try hard. Today he try
to make life like at home.
We look at pictures, then we dine,
and then we see the film.
It is Cocteau. I hear them speak.
En français – my heart lift
to hear the words, the language
of my friends.

'It is enough,' I tell him in the night.
The night his hands reach for me,
and I draw away. 'It is enough
I do as you have say.
I cry no more. I make a friend face
for them all. Do not ask more of me.
This is all I can do. *Ça suffit.*'

Irena, Sunday 6 May 1951

He turn from me this morning.
So I cry.
Never Viktor able turn him from my tears.

We go to eat the breakfast with them
before they go to walk to station –
They are *lutherische*, she tell me,
with church in city. 'And you?' she ask.
I tell her I *catholische*.
'That's Catholic, love.' The man explain her.

'But we go not to church.' She look surprise.
I see the face on daughter. For moment
she look – I need more English words –
she look like she too want not go to church.
She want to be like us, and stay in house.

'I make you coffee,' say the woman, Missus Joe.
I try call her Doss, an ugly name.
Perhaps I say it Doris. That she tell me
is the proper name.

She call this coffee? *To je spainy.*
Not for drinking. I watch her.
From bottle comes this thick black –
like poison. On the bottle: Bushells
Coffee with Chicory. What this may be
I do not know. Only I cannot drink it.

Viktor. His eye on me.
I make myself to swallow.
I am actor, I remember.

Irena, Monday 7 May 1951

My spirit lifting.
Yesterday we go in afternoon
to meet the friend that Viktor make in hostel.

He bring his woman.
She work in big shop in the city
in shoe department – so she tell me.

She looking at my shoes –
I bring from home.
I have bring many shoes.
But still so many have I leave
behind me when we go.

I tell her of my shoes.
Soft leather from Italia.
I tell her of designer
who make shoes for me.

'You want to work?' she ask me.
'We need more people in my place.
I tell my manager.
If you know shoes like this,
I think he has place for you.'

'*Prosim*!' I say her. Please!
Such work! Beneath me, *ja*!
To work in shop.
But this new land, and new ways.
And to get out of house each day…

Doss, Friday 11 May 1951

Well, Madam's got a job, she has.
I tell you, Lizzie, this is a relief.
The problems that I've had this week with her
quite honestly, they'd beggar your belief.
To have her gone each day will be much better
and I can face the evenings – they're not bad
because the rest are with us, and as well
perhaps she won't be always feeling sad!

In fairness I would have to say
I know she's tried this week, that's true.
But even so that snooty way of hers
of watching every single blooming thing I do
as if I'm not quite up to scratch
would be enough to make milk turn.
And then the thing she did the other day
that really made me positively burn
was when she went down to the shops alone –
came back as pleased as punch, with some coffee
some ground-up beans she managed to buy there
and said that now she would teach me
the proper way to make it. Who does she think
she is? A wonder that I didn't spit
right in her face. Instead I tried to smile
and said I'd think about it for a bit.

So when she went to have her interview
I must admit I said a prayer or two.

Claire, Sunday 13 May 1951

Irena has a job. In George's – in their shoe department.
I can see her there. She's so glamorous.
This last week she's been different – real friendly.
She even showed me photos of herself
on stage. Golly, she looked lovely. She wore
a long cloak – reckon it was velvet – and all trimmed
with fur around the neck and down the front.
Her hair was sort of curled in ringlets that cascaded
down her back. Reminded me a bit of when
Mum used to put mine up in curling papers.
I tried to tell Irena about that, but guess she
didn't understand – or maybe wasn't interested.
She's just so beautiful. I love the way
she does her make-up. I wonder if she'd
let me learn from her one day. Maybe even
show me how. It's no wonder that Viktor
watches her the way he does.

And yet sometimes he seems quite sad. It's then
he looks most like a movie star. I'm never sure
which one he's most like. Some days I think
it's Cary Grant, but then on others it's Olivier.
But no, he's thinner – more Sinatra – or perhaps
it's even Humphrey Bogart. Oh, he's the one
who makes me swoon. I'd love to be Lauren Bacall
and have someone look at me just the way he does
at her. 'Cos that's the way that Viktor looks
at Irena. She doesn't seem to notice.

Doss, Monday 14 May 1951

Almost as good as being at the pictures, Lizzie,
when last night at the dinner table
Paul asked the Kasals how they got away.
He said his teacher asked how they were able
to get free from the commies, in a land
where all the borders have been shut.
So Paul was eager to find out; he said
he'd heard you couldn't leave, but
here they were. 'How did you do it?'
was his question. 'Was it very hard?
Was there a fight to get away? With guns?
Wasn't there a border guard?'
Viktor really made it sound quite easy.
He didn't make tremendous song and dance
but still it was exciting. It was clear
that they had really taken quite a chance.
He told us they'd pretended they were going
for holidays in some big country home
Irena's family owned, not too far from the border.
Then a picnic in the forest meant that they could roam
into the woods. They only had with them what they
could carry, and they walked all day till night
when they could manage to avoid patrols
that came with dogs and hunted for a sight
of any Czechs who might be making for the border
into Germany. Each time they saw a light
from torches they would have to stop and wait
until it passed on, and they knew it was all right.
I tell you, Lizzie, though he made it sound
quite easy – we could almost see
how dangerous it was. I'd never really thought
how lucky we are to live in a land that's free.

Claire, Friday 18 May 1951

She said that I could take a photo into school.
I told her that I wanted to show friends what she was like
because she was so glamorous. She laughed.
Her laugh is lovely too. Like little bells, the sort
that tinkle when great ladies are ringing for their maids.
I told Mum that one day. She sniffed.
'I reckon that's just what she thinks she is,' she said.
Mum doesn't understand her. Irena says
some people have been born to be misunderstood.
Well, that's not quite exactly how she put it,
but I knew what she meant. And then she said,
'Some people never understand fine things.'
I think that maybe she meant Mum, and for a minute
I felt angry. But she's right. Mum's different, and
she'll never understand Irena – but I can.

The girls at school thought she was beautiful.
'And does she really live with you?' They treat
me differently now. We've got an actress
living in our house. OK, right now she's selling
shoes, but in a real exclusive shop. I'd love
to go and see her at her work. Maybe one day
she'll let me come and watch her for a while.

Joe, Friday 25 May 1951

I'd have to say
that this has been
a better week.
Viktor seems
a new man too.
I reckon she's
not easy to be with.
Nervy, y'know.
Lots of tears.
But that's been better
since she started
working. Must say
I can't quite picture
her at work. But
she seems happy.
So is Doss.
Got her down –
not like my Doss at all.
Gave her a hug
the other night.
Can't do much more
these days now that
we sleep with kids.
I guess it's not for long.
Hope not. I like
to know she's
next to me at night,
even if there's not
much of the other stuff
these days.

I guess we're getting
older, and that goes.
Not sure how Viktor
feels, though. See him
looking at his missus.
Wonder what it's like
with them.

Viktor, Sunday 27 May 1951

A cloud is lifting from our lives, and for a moment
my heart also lifts. Still it seems amazing to me
to see Irena in this new life. Each day she goes to work.
I wake her as I leave, for Joe and I must walk to reach
the early train. Later, buses start. Good fortune, that.
Irena's shoes would not do well on that long walk
to reach the station. But she rises as I go,
prepares herself as if for some important place
and sets out to the city and her job.
At night so tired. I greet her as she comes.
I try to hold her close. She shakes her head, and swiftly
moves away. 'First I must bathe, and then it will be
time to eat the meal.' I see that with each day
her speech is easier. Soon this language will come
readily for both of us. Perhaps as this new life
becomes our lives, perhaps we find again
our happiness together. I can wait.

Viktor, Friday 1 June 1951

At home, it will be springtime. In the high Tatras
the snows will still be melting, but in the meadows
will be blue and yellow crocuses. In Prague
the Vltava will be in spate, and linden trees will be
in full new green for spring. But now already will be
cherry blossoms ending, and the fresh green leaves
will soon begin to hide the small sour balls of fruit.

I courted her under the cherry blossom.
The first time that she let me take her I remember
was in the orchard on her father's land.
I live that day again so many times.
The checkered rug, wine glasses overturned…
and after it was over, there were white fallen blossoms
on her breasts. My lips brushed them away.
She smiled at me.

Here in this land where everything is different
the trees have lost their autumn leaves. I watch
the colours change – the reds, the golds –
like flames they seemed. They also fell,
but not as blossoms fall. All gone.
The trees now stand unclothed; like skeletons
they raise their arms in supplication to the sky.
A sky which turns unyielding face to them.
Tomorrow will be winter here.

Viktor, Saturday 2 June 1951

She rises from the dinner table quickly, nods her head.
Always she is courteous. Her mother's training
and the manners of our past always will make it so.
Each night she sets off swiftly for our room,
but they are hurt, I know, she does not stay.
Joe's voice is kindly. 'I guess it's tough,' he says.
'Your missus must get pretty tired,
not being used to work and all.' I nod my head,
grateful for his understanding. The woman, Doss,
she makes a small sound, starts to clear the table.
'No need for you to go,' she says. 'Stay and we'll
listen to the news.' We gather round the wireless.
'All helps your English too,' she adds. 'Must say
your wife's is getting better every day.' I wonder
how she knows. Irena speaks so little to her.
But for some time today she's had the girl with her,
and so this may be what the mother thinks of.
Together they have opened boxes that Joe brought in
from the shed. I stood a while, seeing things
but half-remembered from our lives before.
Some treasured pieces, lengths of coloured silk,
a few small pictures. Like children, so excited,
they opened packages that in another life
we'd chosen to come with us to this land.
I watched them: Irena so lovely, flushed with joy,
recalling other days and other ways.
The girl, still just a child, but with the promise
of a time to come. They looked up at me,
standing by the door. 'Oh Viktor,' cried the girl,
'Do come and see the treasures we are finding.'

Claire's smile was warm, and in that moment
she was not a child, and I could see the woman
she would one day be. Irena was impatient,
and quick to silence her. 'These are not matters
for a man,' she said. I turned away.

Irena, Saturday 2 June 1951

The girl have ask me, while we working,
to tell her of the travel from my land.
I shake my head. I do not wish remember.
Bamberg and Delmenhorst – the years we live
in camp, waiting to find country
that will take us. We feel no more like people.
We are animals. They send us here, they send us there.
'Not so,' say Viktor. 'We can choose.'
'Well then, I say America.' For this we must wait
many years, he tell me. But a man has come
and say Australia will offer home, if Viktor
willing to work two years for their government.

I look around at camp. The little room – we have
good luck to be here in own room, to eat good food,
for Viktor has some kitchen work. We take
what UNRO give us – clothes, soap, and cigarettes –
I feel like beggar woman, a gypsy who have
her hand out all time for what others give.
I, Irena Kasals, to live like this.

I do not tell the girl, this Claire, what it feel like
in camp. 'You tell yes this two year work,'
I say Viktor. 'Australia. Any land. Not here.'
They give us papers, and we go on train to north.
Another time like animals we go. Like cattle
on the ship from Bremerhaven. I sleep in bunk
with women and their children. Row on row
of beds – the children up on top, some
four bunk high. They can look down on me.
I wish to scream. When I see Viktor in the day,
he try to hold me, make it better. I push him
from me. He is one who bring me to this.

Claire, Sunday 3 June 1951

This has been such a special weekend. I'd never thought
Irena could be so nice. But when she asked me
if I would like to help unpack some of her boxes
I was so thrilled. We didn't do them all.
She just showed Dad the few she wanted.
Mum had asked me if I wanted to go shopping
with her. I told her that I'd stay home with Irena.
Mum said that she'd be going to the Junction
to look for a new frock. My auntie's getting married
and Mum and Dad will go to that next month.
Kids are not invited. Aunt Maureen lives a long way off –
the country somewhere. Mum hates new clothes. She says
she ought to lose some weight before the wedding.
She won't, I know. She'll get a new perm though.
I love Irena's hair. It's such a lovely colour.
'Bottle blonde,' I heard Mum say to Lizzie.
'Like to know what her real colour is.'
As if it matters.
Irena says she'll teach me about make-up.
She says the secret is to hide what you have done.
She showed me with her rouge – just how
she blends it in around the edges, so that it looks
as if it's only natural colour. I said to her
'Mum doesn't use rouge much, but when she does
it looks as if she's got a fever.' Irena nodded,
but didn't say a word.

Claire, Monday 4 June 1951

'What did you learn at school today?'
Dad put me on the spot tonight at dinner.
I squirmed. That's what he used to do
when I was just a child, at primary school.
You don't do that to people of my age.
But we were sitting silent at the table –
I think he wanted someone to say something.
Then Viktor looked at me, and smiled.
I think he almost winked. As if I was a friend,
and not a kid. I think I must have blushed
'cos Paul put down his fork and looked at me.
'Hey, sis, you've gone real red.'
I told them about art class and the Rembrandts
in the book Miss Arbrey showed us. I've tried
to learn a bit of this stuff lately. Viktor and Irena
know so much. She looked impressed.
Then Viktor said there was a Rembrandt in our gallery.
They'd seen it on their day in town. 'Not perhaps his best,
but still a Rembrandt. A self-portrait.' I was excited.
Maybe it was one of those she'd shown us in the book.
He thought a moment, then he offered
'We could perhaps one day take you to see it?'
I looked at Dad to check. He chewed and nodded.
'Well, that's real good of you.
I'd have to say it's not our cup of tea.
But if you're willing, and you'd like to go there, missy,
say thank you nicely. Talking about tea,
I'm ready for a cuppa, luv.'

Claire, Tuesday 5 June 1951

Can't wait to get to school today, and tell them all
I'm going to the gallery. It's so nice
of Viktor and Irena. Last night I dreamed
about them. Well, actually it was Viktor
that I dreamed about, and we were walking down
a tunnel filled with pictures. Right at the other end
there was a door. Not sure why, but almost felt
it could be scary. Don't know why. Viktor told me
not to worry – in my dream, this is.
I didn't get to open it. But I wonder
what would have been behind the door.

Claire, Blues Interlude 2

I walk along the passageway towards that waiting door.
I walk with trembling knees along the darkened passage to that waiting door.
It looms there all distorted like the fun fair mirror I once saw.

> *It fills my mind with promise and with fear.*
> *I want to run away and not be here.*
> *It beckons yet forbids; how can this be?*
> *I want to open it, but not to see*
> *what may be waiting there for me.*
> *My body throbs with feelings strange and new.*
> *Although I try to stop, I think of you.*

There are gardens of delight beyond that door.
There are perfumed gardens of delight spread out for me beyond that door.
But under flowers lurks a sinuous snake I have not known before.

> *And more intense the promise and the fear.*
> *So much I want to run and not be here.*
> *It beckons yet forbids; how can this be?*
> *If only I could open it, but still not see*
> *what may be waiting there for me.*
> *My body throbs with feelings strange and new.*
> *Although I try to stop, I think of you.*

You watch me coming as I near the door.
You watch with tender eyes and see me shaking as I near the waiting door.
My footsteps falter; filled with fear, I hesitate still more.

Claire, Friday 8 June 1951

Don't think I'll get to sleep tonight. It's tomorrow
that I'm going into town with them. Not just
the gallery, but afterwards we're going to have
coffee at a place they know in Lygon Street.
'It is permitted?' he asked Mum. 'I promise you
we take good care of her.' It made me feel
a little bit as if I'm just a child. But when
he smiled at me, it didn't feel like that – but
more like being someone special. Made Mum
agree to it. Later on she said to me:
'Afternoon tea in town, that's very nice of them.
You *are* a lucky girl. Make sure you mind
your Ps and Qs. Don't want her thinking
you don't know how to behave.'
'Oh, Mum!'

Claire, Sunday 10 June 1951

When I wake up this morning, Mum is out already.
I can hear her in the kitchen, singing.
It's early, so no need to get up yet. Lots of time
for getting ready for the trip to church.
I'll just stay here a bit; I want to think about
the day we had. Really wish that I was still
in my old room. I'd like to lie and watch
the peaches on the wall. They always make me
feel so good. Like little suns. Not that I need
the peaches. I feel happy just thinking
over yesterday. But it wasn't quite the way
I'd thought that it would be. For a minute I was
disappointed when Irena said she'd leave us –
she wanted to go shopping, not spend
her afternoon with paintings, so she'd meet us
afterwards. Viktor shrugged. I love that word.
It's what they do in movies. I could see him
on the Civic screen – the girls at school agreed.
We put him in our dreamboat list. I thought
he might be angry that he was stuck with me,
but he was lovely. Made me feel that he was
actually happy that we had the time
to get to know each other. It was different
being there with him. Not like a school excursion.
We stood in front of pictures while he showed me
just how to look at them. I saw the way the light
caught eyes, and shadows made us see things
that we might have overlooked. I learned to see
more closely how the painter balanced all the parts,
and somehow pictures came alive. No hurry.

He made me stand a long time looking. 'This time
is well spent.' Then he watched me
as I learned to see the way that he had showed me.
'Not many,' he said firmly. 'It is better
to look closely at these few. We will come back
another day.' But I was sorry when we left…
We found Irena waiting, and as he hurried to her
I felt he had forgotten me. Strange feeling.
Almost hurt. Then he turned and touched my arm.
'She learns well. She is perceptive, and her eye
is good.' Irena laughed. 'So too is mine.
I show you what I buy. But first, my coffee.'
They teach me a new word. I learn to call it
cappuccino.

Viktor, Sunday 10 June 1951

These children – touching in their innocence –
it leads me sometimes in these nights to wonder…
Perhaps if we had children, if Irena had been willing,
I wonder if we would have reached this place.

I think not so. With children it would not be possible
to face that journey from our home. But yet,
to stay. To see the work of generations go.
My father's factories. To see that rabble take them
from me. 'It is permitted,' so they told me.
'You are allowed to stay – as manager.'
That was their way. The state would take possession.
We who had made them, we who understood
exactly what was needed – we could remain and watch
the new men take command. And for how long?
I had watched friends each day reduced,
made smaller. Until at last was nothing left of them
or of their work. Now in this new land
there is no way these men can understand. I hear them
at the benches, talking. They speak of things they do not know.
Commies, they call them. There are some indeed
who speak as if this could be good. I hear a lad –
what could he know? – he calls it glorious!
a workers' revolution. He looks towards me,
fingers the red scarf that brushes pimpled skin,
and points nail-bitten fingers. 'You musta seen,'
he jabs towards me, 'You musta seen some stuff.'
I shake my head, and look away. For I have seen
too much that he could never understand.

If we had children, would we still have faced
the journey? And only just in time. The boxes –
these at least had gone. Our friends in Switzerland
were caring for our treasures. But still we lingered, thinking
it might be that we could stay, Irena so unwilling.
But even she could see that night, the Russian soldiers
marching through our streets, that it was time to go.

Tonight I sit. Looking at these children at the table,
so young, so innocent. What of the children I have seen
lying bloodied in the streets of home, or starving
in the gutters? While we, still masters even in
those godforsaken times, still with our factories
and smokestacks belching black, against the lurid skies,
we were the ones who kept the German war machine alive –
or so they, unsuspecting, thought. *Je*, in those days
we could play double games, still prosper.
And even after war, our way of life continued…
until the Russians came. Then innocence was done.
We could no longer shut our eyes.

Viktor, Sunday 10 June 1951

I shut my eyes, but still I see them there.
The children from my land. I walk again
the war-torn streets of Praha. Prague.
Prague the golden city, city of my youth.
City of my memories. City of my dreams.
But how can I recapture golden spires,
when all I see is ragged children, large-eyed,
huddled under broken buildings?
The houses shot at, torched, where Jews have lived.
The little girl they threw in on the fire...
They haunt my dreams.
But is it better for them now?
Where are they in this worker-state?

The children of this land are innocent.
They have not seen the ravages of war.
This boy, who makes his toys the model planes,
he has not seen them come, death-dealing,
from the skies. When he runs the length of hallway
and makes the noise of gunfire, he is not one
who has to shrink and fear that sharp staccato sound.

I shut my eyes, and try to make them disappear.
Beside me in the bed Irena murmurs in her sleep.
To take her in my arms – what comfort that would be.
But then to feel her move away, feel her withdraw...
I think instead about the day. The girl –
another innocent – but something there.

I watch her with the paintings, see her face,
flushed with pleasure. The moment when she turns
towards me, eyes shining with delight,
because she sees things now she has not seen before.
This we will do again. To give new vision
to a fresh untutored mind, a special pleasure.
I focus on her face to blot the other out.

Claire, Monday 11 June 1951

The others asked me all about it. At the lockers,
Pamela waiting for me. 'Tell us everything.
What was it like?' I actually didn't want to say
that he and I had looked at pictures on our own.
It was too special somehow. I didn't want
them joking, making funny faces, the way we do
whenever we think someone may be keen
on somebody. Not that I am, of course.
It's just that Saturday belongs to me.
Even thinking now about it makes me glad
I didn't share it with the other girls.
So I only told them how we went for coffee
in that little shop in Lygon Street.
'An Eyetie place?' said Joan. And sniffed.

Joe, Friday 15 June 1951

Kind-hearted chap, Viktor.
Bet he would have liked
kids of his own.
Bet that it was her doing
that they didn't.
You can tell.
I've seen him
with young Paul.
Real patient with the kid.
Helped him
the other night
make that new Spitfire
Paul had saved
his pocket money for.

Says they'll take
Missy to the gallery again.
She's learning things
from them that we can't
teach her. She's a
bright button, that one.
Might even get
to university,
her teachers say.

Irena, Saturday 16 June 1951

I wake today with headache, migraine.
This every day on feet in shop too hard.
But people kind. The manager say me
I godsend. Lend department class.
Not hard. His other women cows,
but kind to me because I foreigner.
They know not what I thinking
of them. I am actress; Viktor right.

Mein Gott: a train each morning.
I, Irena Kasals, on train.
And first, before this train is bus.
I think sometime my mother…
Her words, if now she see me.
In shop is different. There I queen.

Today the migraine. So today I sleep.
Let Viktor take the little one to city.
This place a city? Ah, they not know
city as we do. Berlin, before the war,
unter den Linden in the night-time,
Paris, with her flowers – Viktor buy me
flowers from women on the river bank –
Milano where each year we go to opera –
and our own Praha, still so golden
until the Russkis come.

I look at streets of Melbourne, and I think
these people never have know cities, or
they could not think this one.

Claire, Sunday 17 June 1951

It's almost better, in a funny sort of way,
when it's just two of us. I wondered,
when Irena got up sick, and said she couldn't come,
if that would mean the whole trip would be off.
I'd started on my project, and it would have been a pity
not to get back to the gallery on Saturday.
But Viktor said that he would take me on my own –
if Mum and Dad did not object. For half a minute
Mum looked as if she might say no. But then
Dad said, 'Don't let her be a nuisance
if you've other things to do.' But Viktor smiled
and told him that he thought it was important
that I saw more before I wrote up my report.

Important. I like to think about that word.
It has a good feel to it. It's nice to be
important.

Today Irena says she'll show me photographs,
the pictures of their home in Prague – she
calls it Praha, then remembers that I won't know
what she means. I asked at school about it
and the lady in the library found me papers –
different ones, not like the *Sun* or *Argus* –
these had long articles, quite hard to understand.
All about the way the communists had taken
people's land and factories. When I asked Viktor
he said it was true. His brother had a factory – well, factories
was what he said – that made the loveliest glass,
and sent all sorts of things to countries everywhere.
'Even here?' I questioned him. He shook his head.

But everywhere in Europe. And then the state had taken
all his brother's factories – and all of his. It seems
unfair. How can a government take things
that people have worked hard to get?
We talked about it all the afternoon.
He doesn't treat me like a child.

Irena, Sunday 17 June 1951

This house, this room, so ugly.
On Saturday I have look it. I see
how it lack style. It have no grace.
I show to Claire the pictures of our home.
She see our life there on Vitkova Street –
she ask me, 'So big house? Who cares for it?'
I tell her of the maids, the garden workers,
the man who drive Viktor to factory each day
and then me where I wish to go.
I tell her of the city, of Hradcany Castle,
Cathedral and the Charles Bridge with the statues.
Almost I see them when I talk; soon each breath hurt
and I am near to tears. My father's country house,
then Viktor's, mine...all gone.

'The war?' she ask.

'Not war. A little bombing, yes.
But not like other places. No, after war.
Not soon. Some years life start to be again
the way we have known it. But then come Russians
and all changes. We can see what will be.'

And so we go. She knows how we escape.
She asks me, if we can take nothing, how it is now
that we have these things. I try to tell her of the *paserak*,
the man who will take risks, for money take our goods
across the borders. To Austria, and Switzerland. Our friends
in other lands, who keep these boxes for us.
Her face is puzzle. She does not understand.
'But why would they not let you take your things?'

How could she understand? I shake my head.
'Another day, *mílácek*. Not today.'

Today I open other box and think
what I can do to make this place
not so much ugly.

Doss, Monday 18 June 1951

A funny old weekend it's been.
Madam in her room. We've scarcely seen
her out with us at all. I really couldn't call
this anything but better, but for all
that I'm not absolutely fussed
about the way that she and Viktor just
about seem to have Claire obsessed.
When Missy's not at school, the rest
of her free time she seems to spend
with Kasals. There's no end
to it. She's either with them, or she tells
me non-stop what they say. How Mrs K sells
lovely shoes, how elegant her dress
(by contrast I feel a real mess)
about their homes before they came here…
The other day I said to her, 'Look dear,
you really mustn't bother them so much.'
She simply looked at me: 'Irena says I'm such
a comfort to her…' Well, what can I do?
It's almost that somehow those foreign two
have taken over what's my house and child.
Enough to drive a woman properly wild!

Doss, Friday 29 June 1951

I'd felt quite sorry for her when she came
wet and bedraggled back tonight. You couldn't blame
her for bad temper. She'd had a long hard day.
But just when you are feeling sorry, such a way
she has of making you feel very small…
It's partly how she stands there, proud and tall,
and looks at me as if I'm dirt
beneath her feet. I tell you, I get hurt.
I thought they were supposed to be
saving money for a place, well that's what he
keeps saying; wonder if she knows!
The way she spends her money! Mainly clothes.
As Lizzie puts it, a clothes horse…
I don't think Viktor would be one to force
her to stop spending. After all, he'd say,
she earns her money, and this for her is a hard way.
Mind you, I don't think that she's worked before.
I guess it's hard to understand that now you're poor.

Claire, Sunday 1 July 1951

Irena's made my room so beautiful. I really can't see
why Mum's so upset. Not that she said much to her,
but we knew that she was mad. I helped Irena with it.
She'd bought some lovely things – material she hung
across the bookshelves – velvety – and other
filmy delicate stuff – it was gorgeous – that she had
in sort of drapes around the walls. Same colours
as the new bedspread, all dark and glowing. I could see
how different it looked. She took the other bedspread off
and folded it real neatly, and told me I should take
the old one back to Mum. I didn't like to let her know
that Mum had bought it specially for them.
Mum's face went red. 'Not good enough for Madam,
I suppose!' I really hate the way she calls Irena
'Madam' when she's angry. That's most of the time.
Irena bought a lamp – it makes the whole room glow.
Then she unpacked some boxes and got out
the loveliest things. She put them on the mantelpiece.
There were some masks – she said they came from Venice –
and eggs, all carved with pictures – Fabber something –
very special things, she told me, worth a lot.
Her family had owned them more than a hundred years.
When we let Viktor in, at first he was quite grim
and asked what she had spent. There was an awful minute
when I thought that she would cry. She looked
just like a disappointed child. But then he took her
in his arms, and said what she had done was wonderful.
She'd made Aladdin's cave. I know that story,
and I reckon he was right.
Mum doesn't think so, though.

Viktor, Sunday 1 July 1951

To see her face alight and happy – it is worth
the money that she spends. Always it has been
so. For her the life must not be ugly. She needs
a place with beauty. I knew we could not stay
in our own land. There will be no more beauty there.
And even all that we have suffered in these nightmare years –
the flight, the camps, the train, the ship –
all this she could survive, in hope of better times.
So how could I deny her these few things,
a chance to make again, in this one room, our past?
I drew her close to me. I thought, perhaps,
with these familiar things, she too might turn to me.
She rested for a moment there, but then I felt
that silken body slip away, to leave me aching
once more with the need. 'Not here, *láska*,
not here.' 'But when, Irena? When? And where?'

Joe, Monday 2 July 1951

Not sure
if we can keep
this going.
A nervy sort, Irena.
Highly strung.
Never thought
I'd see another woman
get Doss's back up
like she can.

Had to calm Doss down
after the bedspread
came back.
She seemed to take it
personal-like.
Never understand
the way that women-folk
see things. It's strange.

But Viktor tries
to smooth things over.
Praises Doss's cooking.
That goes down well.

Claire, Thursday 5 July 1951

We talk a lot more these days round the dinner table.
Dad always reads the paper on the trip home,
and he and Viktor talk about the news. It's good.
Sometimes I can join in, and Miss McGinty says
my history work is getting better. In fact,
my end of term report said that I showed
a 'growing understanding'. Guess that happens
when you live with people who have seen
a world you didn't know about before.
We listen to the wireless after dinner, and
even Mum sometimes says something about
what is happening in the world. Not if
Irena's there, though. Most nights Irena goes straight
to their room and takes her coffee with her.
When I've done my homework, I go there;
we read the fashion magazines she buys.
Mum says that *Women's Weekly* does for her.

I think you'd call Irena cultured. I have an idea now
what that word means. I want to be
like that. One day I will be cultured too.
Viktor says that I learn quickly, that I have
a natural good taste. A funny way of putting it –
good taste. I like it, though.

Claire, Saturday 7 July 1951

They didn't take me out with them today.
I really missed it. It's been lovely
doing things with them each Saturday.
Even the concerts – though I found the music
hard to understand at first.
Today they went out with their friends, and even
got a taxi home – just fancy. It was very late.
I guess the trains had all stopped running.
It woke me up when they came in –
I think that there was something wrong.
It sounded as if they were arguing.
It got quite loud – not shouting, but real close.
And then it went all quiet, and I just about am sure
that it was crying I could hear. I guess
it must have been Irena. Men don't cry, do they?

Claire, Sunday 8 July 1951

They never come to breakfast Sunday mornings. Mum says
that works out well, us being in a rush to get away.
It takes a while to walk down to the station, 'cos buses
don't run Sundays, and if we missed that train
we wouldn't get to church at all. So when they said
that they would sleep late Sundays, and get something
for themselves when they got up, she wasn't fussed a bit.
Didn't stop her saying that the way Irena left the kitchen
showed she wasn't used to cooking, though.

This morning it was different. We could hear Viktor
in the hall, and then he asked Mum if she'd make
a cup of tea for him. And one that he could take Irena.
'Will she drink tea?' Mum asked him, and she had
a funny sort of look. 'I do not know,' he told her,
'But I try.'

Joe, Wednesday 11 July 1951

The poor cove's tried.
You have to hand it
to him. He's looking
all the time for
somewhere else for them.
He gets the paper
every day to hunt.
He goes round shops
and looks at all the ads
they put on little cards
in windows.
But when he gets there
it's always the same answer.
'No rooms left.'
Keeps reminding me
of Bethlehem –
the story of the inn.
Not quite the same,
I know. But tough like that.

We hadn't thought
it would take quite so long
for them to find a place.
But somehow
we can stick it out.
I think.

Claire, Saturday 14 July 1951

This afternoon they took us to play tennis. Well,
really it was Paul, I s'pose – he's learning it
at school. When Viktor heard, he was excited.
His face came all alight. He told us how he used to play
with Drobny. Even Mum and Dad knew who that was.
'My goodness,' Mum was real impressed, 'you mean
that chap in all the papers?' Irena nodded.
'Yes, Viktor play with Jaroslav in club,' she said.
He laughed. 'But never would I win. He has been leader
of our country's team to be the champions in Europe.'
'Wonder if you'd give our Paul some tips?' asked Dad.
So that was why they took us down to Glendale Road
this afternoon. They looked like people in a magazine.
Irena had a proper tennis dress – she bought it yesterday –
and Viktor… He was smashing. I felt so stupid
in my school sports skirt, until he looked at me
and told me that I was a young Diana.
I'm not sure who she was; I'll hunt it up
on Monday in the library. He coached us for a while;
Irena watched us from the lawns. And then they played
together. I think that it's the first time that I've seen
Irena laughing, really happy. They're so good.
Even with old racquets from the club hire, you could see
that they were good. And people came to watch them.
I looked at him, and there was something in me
almost hurting. He let me hold his jumper and his towel.
And when they finished, Viktor came to sit with me;
we walked back up the hill together while he told me
about his Drobny match back home in Prague.

Doss, Sunday 15 July 1951

Joe, does it ever bother you
to see the way that Claire
is spending all her time?
I'll swear she's always there
with the Kasals. I hardly see
my daughter any more.
At night she does her lessons,
then she hears the door –
Irena's home; she's off –
this happens every night.
And even when you men get here
we hardly get a sight
of her. It's all she talks about:
Irena this, Irena that. I'm sick
and tired of it, you know.
She really is too thick
with them, particularly her.
It makes me wonder just why they
put up with it. Perhaps because
they don't quite want to say
to her that she's a pest.
But then I must admit
Irena brings it on herself –
in fact she seems to welcome it.
Claire's changing, Joe.
We're losing her, you know.
I'll really welcome it when they
have somewhere else to go.

Irena, Thursday 19 July 1951

One day more, then this week over.
This place, this people. I come here
each night and think myself
how much more can I bear?
This woman's food on table –
so heavy, dull, like her. We sit
at table and I look at them.
Each day on shop floor, stupid talk,
and silly women wanting shoes
they have not proper feet for.
Then crowded train and bus
and here this house. And Viktor
with his long sad face. He seem
to like these people. He talk
to Joe, and even to the woman.
He praise her food – Viktor
who has known the dishes of our home
and restaurants in Rome, Madrid.
We who eat Sachertorte in Salzburg
patisserie in Paris,
now see each Monday shepherd's pie.
Food for sheep herders, yes. But not for me.
I put aside the knife and fork.
The girl is watching me. I smile
a little in myself when she also put down
her fork and say, 'Not really hungry, Mum.'

Claire, Saturday 21 July 1951

Most Saturdays Irena has to work till lunch. But
not today; she stayed in bed till very late.
I waited to see her come out to the bathroom,
looking just so elegant. She has this gown –
a negligée she calls it. It's red and silky.
It's trimmed all down the front
with something white and soft and feathery.
I told the girls at school – we found
a picture like it in a magazine. I said
Irena actually looked much prettier.
'Not very practical,' Mum criticised. Well,
her old flannel one is nothing like Irena's –
that's for sure. Some day I'm going to have
the sorts of clothes Irena has. She says
she'll take me shopping one day with her.
But not today. This afternoon while she is shopping
I'm going to the gallery with Viktor.
I love these afternoons. What's even better,
he seems to like them too. That's what he said.
I think about that in the nights.

Claire, Saturday 28 July 1951

Today was just so different. I guess that it was Mum
who started it. At breakfast time she looked at me
and Paul, and said we didn't play together any more.
I mean to say, he's just a little boy!
'You used to always do so much at weekends.'
'But, Mum, those days we were just little kids.'
'You used to love the creek.' That's true.
We did. We used to go adventuring
along the banks. Amazing what we'd find.
All sorts of things. Almost a rubbish dump
but full of treasures. 'Tell me about it,'
Viktor asked me, smiling. So we described
the way we'd scramble down the banks
and walk along the tracks and play all sorts
of games – it really used to be a lot of fun.
'I too had country childhood,' Viktor said.
'I wish to see your creek.' That was the start.

A different Saturday. 'You'll need old clothes,'
I warned him. It's muddy at the edges.
'I have old shoes.' Dad looked a bit surprised.
He's never thought to come adventuring with us.
Somehow I couldn't see Dad clambering down
the crumbling edges to reach the grassy bit –
but Viktor did. And helped me when it got
too steep. I could have done it on my own,
but didn't want to say so. His arm around me
somehow felt so nice. Then when we
got to that part with the oak trees we sat down.
Paul soon got bored and wandered off, but we
stayed there a long long time. Even though
it's winter, there were still some leaves and, when
the wind blew, dry brown scraps came floating down.
Some landed on my head, but Viktor picked them off.
They'd tangled in my hair. He took a long time,
then he touched my cheek so softly it was like
another leaf had landed on it.

Claire, Sunday 29 July 1951

Something's changed. I'm not sure what.
I look at Viktor; inside me there's something
different from the way I felt before.
It's like I'm breathing harder, and I think about
the feather touch of his hand on my cheek.
I want to feel it there again.
Last week Pam asked me in the lunch hour
whether we still had DPs living with us.
We were sitting as we always do – Pam and Beverley,
and Monica and Alison and me – we've been
good friends since state school days –
we tell each other everything. Most times.
'You never talk about them any more,' she said.
The wind was cold, and we were huddled up
against the cream brick wall outside the science block.
It's been our spot for lunchtime all this year.
The others were all looking at me now. I think
perhaps my cheeks were red. But that was probably
because it was so cold. I knew I should have
got my coat before we went outside for lunch.
'You used to talk about them all the time,' she said.
'Yes, they're still there,' I said. Then Beverley
joined in. 'Do they still take you out on Saturdays?'
'Sometimes,' I told them. 'Not every week.'
'Well? We all thought that you might be
a bit keen on him." I tried to laugh at that.
'Come off it. He's quite old.' And then
the bell rang for the end of lunch. We hurried in
to get books from our lockers. I've never been so glad
to go back into class.

Joe, Wednesday 1 August 1951

Women worry.
Can't really understand
what's bothering Doss.
Seems to me
that Kasals have been good
for Claire. She's doing
so much better now at school.
She's growing up.
Must say, it's true,
the things that int'rest her
these days
are way beyond me.
They took her to the ballet
a few weeks ago. Can't see
the sense of all that
jumping round a stage, myself.
Told her so. 'Oh, Dad!'
she said and sort of sighed.
They seem to like
to have her with them.
Guess it's because
they don't have nippers
of their own.
'Well, these are ours –
not theirs,' said Doss.

Doss, Friday 3 August 1951

About that wedding, Lizzie,
you know the one that I
told you about last month –
Joe's sister, well, half-sister really by
his dad years after his mum died…
I think I've told you how
his dad remarried later on.
Joe doesn't see much of them now.
He didn't feel that close to her
but says we really ought to go
now that she's getting married.
I simply don't quite know…
It's leaving kids at home,
especially as you'll be away.
Joe says with Kasals there it's fine.
OK – if it was just a day
I wouldn't worry, but whether train
or car it will be hours on the road.
We'll have to stay two nights.
That's quite a load
to burden strangers with,
even ones who live with you.
But children aren't invited
so what else are we to do?

Irena, Sunday 5 August 1951

So come another week. We go today – again –
to look for home. We go from house to house.
Viktor, he say to them we need house very bad.
Woman shake head. Man say, 'Room gone.'
Just one who tell us, 'Yes, is possible.'
We look at room – such dirt I have not see.
And then rat jump from corner, and I scream.
We catch tram in the city. Silent. Sit all way
with not one word. Viktor shoulder down.
Almost I think to reach and touch his hand.
But something stop me. So I look
from window. See houses where lights come
to show that somewhere there is life.
Back to this place, and room I try to make
my own.

Joe, Sunday 5 August 1951

Poor blighter's almost
had enough, I think.
It's tough for them,
to go out every week
and find that everywhere
there's nothing to be had.
Think there's a chance
he might be having
one or two drinks
in his room at night.
They know that we're
no drinkers here.
I saw too much of what it did
to my old dad
those years just after
Mum was gone.
Swore I'd never put
a kid of mine through that.
That's not to say
that I'd blame Viktor, though.
I reckon that he's got
enough to make a man
turn to the bottle.
Never seen him worse
for it, however.

Claire, Sunday 5 August 1951

Irena didn't come to Sunday tea. A pity.
Mum had made a special sponge – her ginger fluff.
But Viktor had two pieces, and it wasn't just
to please her. He really likes her cooking.
I think we were all happy just to see him
eating. There was something different about him –
I'm not sure what. He seemed so down.
After tea he came into the lounge room; I was
doing homework and he sat and talked about it
for a while. I wanted to say something nice
to make him feel a bit less awful. You could see
how miserable he felt. But for some reason
I just couldn't find the words. And anything
we talked about felt funny. Finally I said
'I wish you could find somewhere else to live,'
and then I went bright red, because it sounded awful.
He looked at me. 'You want us gone.'
His voice was almost dead. I could have cried.
I shook my head, and then did what I'd wanted to
the whole time we'd been talking. I put my hand
on his, and simply said, 'I love it with you here.'

Viktor, Monday 6 August 1951

There is an innocence about the girl. She does not know
yet how to deal with men. She does not understand
yet what is possible. There was one moment there
last night I could have held her close. There was
a wish in me for comfort, and that loving touch
with little trouble could have led to more.
I would not so betray her father's trust.
Instead, the lonely bed. Irena's body turned away.

Claire, Wednesday 8 August 1951

Enid's had experience, they say. We talk about it sometimes
in the cloakroom. Matric girls say that Enid's done it all.
They said she's gone the whole way with her boyfriend, Eddie.
She must have told them that herself. How else
would they know? I wonder just exactly what it means.
Mum has a book. She said she'll show me when I'm 16.
Not sure why that has to be the age, but I could
always talk to Enid, I suppose. I can't imagine
Mum and Dad…but then I guess they must have done it
sometime – otherwise there wouldn't be a Paul and me.
Pam has a boyfriend from another school. He's older, too.
One day she had a funny mark just near her ear. We asked
her if she had been bitten, and she laughed. Then said
she's had to tell him not to go too far. I found her later,
asked her what she meant. She wouldn't say. So then
I asked her how he made her feel. 'Sort of tingly,'
was the way she put it. 'I get all hot and bothered.'
But she wouldn't tell me any more.
I think I know what she was saying.

Irena, Friday 10 August 1951

They look me – all others in this shoe shop.
No! They have teach me this is not way to say name.
Is Footwear Salon. I shut the eye –
these women do not know what salon is.
They look me and they make the face
when he have lunch each day with me
in staff canteen. This name I learn. Food there
so like what she have put on table every night
it make me feel too sick to look at it.
Then he have come one day and stand close by
and shake the head. 'I understand,' he say.
'But you must eat, or else you cannot work.'

I think at first because he boss he worry only
over job. But then he come again, next day,
then every day he sit at lunch with me.
He talk to me. He tell me where he travel
back in old time before war. Even has he seen
my country, and we talk of Praha and of Paris.

He ask me yesterday where now I live.
I tell him of the house and how I go each night
on train and bus long way to get there.
He say not far from where his home, that he
can take me in his car. I think is very kind.

I do not tell the women in the Footwear Salon.
Or they make more the face.

Claire, Tuesday 14 August 1951

I always look out through the window
to see Irena when she comes. I listen for her key
as she walks in through the front door. These days
it's dark already, though they're starting to get longer.
I think she came home earlier tonight – I guess
she caught the early train.
I watch her through the lounge room door; not spying really –
I just like seeing how she does things, so that
one day I can be like her. She always comes inside
then goes straight to the hall stand in the passage.
It has a mirror, and she stays there quite a while
most nights and checks out how she looks. Tonight
she tried her hair a different way, and swept it up
and to one side. Reminded me of someone
in the movies. Veronica, I think – it could be Lake.
A blonde like her, and just as glamorous. And then
she ran her tongue over her lips, and studied them.
Dad and Viktor were out in the back garden. She
heard them coming in, and quickly went off
to her room. Funny. I always think of it
as hers. It doesn't seem like 'theirs'.
It's certainly not mine. She's even covered over
the ventilator holes above the bed. She says
the sunlight on the walls just bothered her
on mornings when she could sleep in.
I didn't tell her that I loved to see the peaches there.
I thought that she might laugh at me.
I didn't think she'd understand.

Viktor, Friday 17 August 1951

I look at her and wonder. She is not the same.
I have known always when there is someone else.
But yet… How is this possible? We live here
and each day she goes to her work. It is not
the way we were at home, when there were many times
she was alone. I have known that in those days
she was too much without me. My fault. Too much
I was away, in other places, other countries. Mea culpa.
But now, now we are here, I feel so often
that I am the one who is alone.

Irena, Sunday 19 August 1951

Alive. I am alive. I feel at last excitement. All these weeks
I have feel only dead. Tomorrow will be new day
and new week. For Robert drive me home each night.
I say him, 'Not to house. Stop car at corner.'
He understand me. I no want others looking,
thinking what is not. First night I say
I have catch early train because we close shop early.
But other nights we have stop car and sit and talk
before we get to house. I need have nothing
to explain. He tell me that we meet at car.
No causing gossip – what is gossip? I have ask.
He laugh and say I am enchanting. What is this?

Irena, Wednesday 22 August 1951

She come to me in morning, when they go
to ladies' room to smoke. 'You watch yourself,
my girl,' she say. 'You not the first, you know.'
I look her, say, 'I understand not what you mean.'
'You know!' she say, and go with other women.

Joe, Friday 24 August 1951

Went to the flicks
tonight. Always like
a Friday outing
with the family.
Specially when there's
something really funny on.
We walked the half mile
to the Civic – I tucked
my elbow under Doss's
arm – nice feeling, that.
Viktor came along.
Poor coot was at
a loose end. His missus
has to work late
Friday nights. They're
doing stocktake.
He'd planned to go
down to the station, meet
the last train, but she said
no, one of the girls
who had a car would
drive her home.
Frosty night when we
walked back. You could see
stars twinkling in the black –
looked very close. Doss
snuggled up to me.
Felt sorry when I looked
at Viktor on his own.

But then I saw that he
and Paul and Claire
were all together,
magging on about the movie,
so he didn't seem too lonely.

Claire, Friday 24 August 1951

I don't think I can get to sleep tonight. I only want
to think about that walk home. Dad set the pace –
he always walks real fast on Friday nights – and
Viktor, Paul and I trailed after. We were talking,
mainly about movies, this and that. I guess
I wasn't watching properly where I stepped,
because I almost fell into a gutter. Viktor reached out
just to steady me, and took my hand.
'But so so cold,' he said. 'Where is your glove?'
and then he held my hand the whole way home.

I didn't tell him it was in my pocket.

Viktor, Saturday 25 August 1951

If one could know…if one could know for sure.
And yet perhaps it is so. A stocktake? It is possible.
It seems to me another world, a world I once knew well.
We did it also, kept some women back,
we needed help to get the figures right,
we often asked most valued workers to stay late.
So it is possible. Her eyes would not meet mine,
and when they did there was that open gaze
that tells me more than any of her lies.
I could not bring myself to say, 'Irena,
who is he?' Because I still must tell myself,
it may be possible…another stocktake.

Viktor, Sunday 26 August 1951

So easy it would be to let thought stop,
to find a comfort in the friendship
of these people. There is in them
a simple goodness. There is no grey
for these. Black and white alone.
They do not know the things
that we have known. Yet the girl is different.
In her one can sense something
that is more like us. Not so simple.
Less straightforward. She stirs in me
a feeling that is new. A father feeling,
I had thought. I had assured myself she is
the daughter that we do not have.
I am no longer clear; I do not know myself
as surely as I should. The walk back
from the cinema – so easy would it be
for my arm to have drawn her to me.
So hard to keep that hand of simple friendship
holding her cold fingers, while my own
trembled with a feeling I did not expect.
This is Irena's doing; a man can bear only so much.
This must not be; she is a child. And it is
as a child that I must see her.

Doss, Wednesday 29 August 1951

I tell you, Lizzie, I'm upset
and just for once I can't tell Joe.
He's Viktor's mate, and he'd just get
himself all worried. That's no
good to anyone. The other night
I had to nip down to the shop –
I'd started pancakes; found I was right
out of milk – didn't want to stop
midstream, to find a kid, so thought
it would be quicker if I went
myself. Got to the shops and bought
the things I needed; as always spent
more than I'd planned, but I was keen
to finish dinner so ran home real fast
past something I'd much rather not have seen –
I'd crossed the road but when I passed
the bus stop on the corner there I saw a car.
The street lamp lit a woman and a man.
I know I wasn't close, but not too far
to recognise her, so for sure I can
say it was her, Irena, sitting there –
you'd know her any time with that blonde hair.
But who the man might be is anybody's guess.
I think that things with those two are a mess!

Irena, Friday 31 August 1951

He think that he can do this. Another stocktake,
he have say. Another Friday night that I must work.
Another night we go together. Then he bring me back
to corner where we part. He say goodbye;
he give me gift. He think me what?
A common woman. One he can say goodbye, no more,
and give some pretty gift to? So when next week come
I am one more woman on shop floor to see him start
with other girl? He treat me like a whore –
that word I have learn here. I think on him
and feel not clean. His grunting, sweating body
on me; sound that he make. What have I do
with such a pig? Not man. So now
I must go into house and say I have work late.
See Viktor look me. I think he know.
But never will he say. So now the anger in me
rise and choke me. I want only escape this place.

Doss, Wednesday 5 September 1951

Not sure what's up with Madam at the moment.
Been out of sorts all week, a bear with a sore head!
And even snappy when she's with our Claire.
And Sunday she spent all the day in bed.
I'm really not sure what is up.
Is Mrs Kasals sick? I asked him straight.
He looked at me and sighed. 'She is too tired
from work. I hope we only need to wait
and soon she will feel better.' I think
he's feeling that a few days' rest
will fix up what is wrong. I've got my own ideas
but keeping my mouth shut I think is best.

Claire, Friday 7 September 1951

There's something wrong. Irena's been so strange,
not like herself at all the last few days. I'm almost scared
to go to call her, when Mum says it's time for dinner.
She's sitting in her room, just staring at the wall.
At least she doesn't have to work back late tonight.
I guess the stocktake's finished. I asked Viktor yesterday
and he said, 'Yes, I think it's over now.'
He was sitting on the back veranda, sort of hunched
over in the deckchair; he had a glass
of something in his hand. I think that it was wine,
but then he put it down too fast to see. He pointed
to the other chair, and asked me to sit down
and tell him all about my day. We've had exams;
I'd wanted to ask him about the Latin paper.
He's helped me such a lot – he'd studied it
at school, and in a university, he said. But when
I brought the question paper to him, we didn't really
look at it. I'm not sure what we talked about.
I just kept feeling that he looked so sad. I pulled
my chair real close so he could see the paper with me,
but it was more because the feeling that it gave me,
to be brushing up against him, was so special.
I really didn't want to go inside, but when Mum
called us, he got up quite fast and moved away.
I stayed there till she called again; I wanted to keep still
and just hold on to how he makes me feel.

Claire, Saturday 8 September 1951

It was a terrible dinner. I've never seen Mum so upset.
I mean, I've never seen her cry before. But now she's
sitting in our bedroom, and she's cried and cried.
Her hanky looks like a wet washer. And in the other room
Irena is much worse. I'd have to say that she is
almost screaming. I think the word's hysterical.

I'm still not sure just how it started.
Mum had made her shepherd's pie. Again. She makes it
once a week, although I think she knows Irena doesn't like it.
Last night I watched her push the forkfuls round and round
her plate, although she wasn't eating. Mum's face was grim.
She took the plates away into the kitchen and I heard her
scrape Irena's into the chooks' bucket. (Dad often says
our chooks eat just as well as we do. That's why the grocer
always likes to buy our eggs.) I went to help Mum
dish up pudding. She'd stewed some peaches and there was
ice cream too. It looked quite pretty – all that gold
and white. But when we started eating, Irena just put down
her spoon and looked at Mum and told her that she never
could eat – Mum says the word was 'compost'. I'm
not absolutely sure. Mum was just so angry. She got up;
for an awful moment I thought that she might even
throw her plate at Irena. She said she'd never been
insulted quite so badly. Especially, she went on,
by someone like Irena, someone no better than she should be.
I don't know what she meant, but then Irena got to her feet too,
and started crying. Viktor put his arm around her.
'Steady on now, Doss,' said Dad. Mum simply
took no notice. She stood and watched them go. Irena was
just sobbing. Viktor looked distressed, and kept on saying,
'Sorry, sorry,' and shook his head as he went after her.
It was a horrible night.

Joe, Sunday 9 September 1951

I reckon that
it had to happen.
There's been trouble
brewing now for weeks.
I still don't know
for sure
just what the word was.
Viktor swears
his wife did not say
compost.
He says the word was
compôte.
That's what they call
our stewed fruit
when they make it
in their country.
Funny word:
compôte.
Anyone can hear
it sure does sound
like compost.
I can see why Doss
got so upset.
Viktor was almost in tears himself,
could hardly speak.
Nearly forgot his English.
Kept saying,

'*Ne, ne*. She never would
say such a thing. She never
would make insult like that
to your wife. You who so good
to us.
Prominte. I so sorry.'
Could've been quite funny
to hear the way
his words got jumbled up.
He speaks real well
most of the time.
It made it clear
just how upset he was himself.
The words *are* different, though;
it wouldn't have been bad
to say she didn't eat
compôte. If that was
what she really said…

Doss, Tuesday 11 September 1951

Perhaps I did come on too strong…
I don't regret it, though.
She can explain it all she likes
but I'm real certain that I know
what word she used. *Compost!*
Garbage! I won't have her call
my cooking garbage. There's no way
she can apologise for that, and all
I see is that she's sticking to her guns.
I'm pretty sure she isn't going to try
to make things up with me. Last night he came
to tell us sorry, but they'd been to buy
a little stove, electric, for their room. He asked
if it would be okay. They plan
to cook on that. Well, let them. If that is what
they want I sure won't interfere: they can!
Next thing you know they'll set the house on fire.
I hope they don't think that the bit of rent they pay
is going to come down. I tell you that it didn't even cover
what it cost us just to keep them day by day.
Joe says I really had no call to say
the things to her I did.
But then he didn't see the car that night.
Yet maybe there are things that should be hid?

Claire, Saturday 15 September 1951

It's been a horrible week. Mum's still so angry.
Irena doesn't look at her; she just walks in the door,
goes straight into the bedroom, starts that little stove
she's bought, and makes their dinner on it. I think
it's interesting food. She goes up to the markets
and buys stuff in her lunch hour. The other night
she had some funny little dumpling things. I thought
they looked peculiar, but when she gave me one
they really were delicious. I didn't tell Mum, though.
Irena says that I can eat with them whenever I want to.
Somehow I don't think it would be a good idea…
Last night Mum had a pot roast on; when Dad and Viktor
came home, they stood inside the door and smelled it
cooking – Viktor looked quite longingly towards our kitchen.
Dad said, 'You're welcome any time.' He'd seen the look
on Viktor's face. But Viktor only shook his head.
'Women!' they both agreed. After we've had dinner
and cleared everything away, and gone in to the wireless,
then Irena comes, and washes up their dishes in the kitchen.
At least Irena isn't angry with me. She still likes me
to come and talk to her at night. She often gives me things;
last night it was the loveliest scarf. And Tuesday night
a tiny bottle with some real exotic perfume. I thought
it might be for my birthday, but that's still another week to go.

Irena, Sunday 16 September 1951

I feel in trap. I am like hare
in forest in my father's lands.
This country like a barren place.
No soul in city; the people here
like monkey in the zoo.
Today we go to zoo. We take the girl –
Viktor idea. I think he want not be
alone with me. We ask the boy,
but he go to a friend house.
I stand long time, and look at
tiger in the cage. I know
just how he feel. He trapped like me.
Like tiger I have enemy.
At work place other women.
Now they make the laugh.
'You not the first, love,' say one woman.
'He allus try the new ones.'
Her words are scar inside my soul.
And in the house the woman.
The night she tell me that she know.
I never do forgive her that.
I keep the girl – she wish to stay with me.
I will be tiger, even in this cage.

Viktor, Sunday 16 September 1951

Irena. They should have chosen other names for you.
You are the sirens with their singing, and I Odysseus.
Like him I will not stuff my ears with wax, but neither
will I let them bind me to the mast. You are Arachne
and I watch you spin your web, unable to tear it
apart. For now I see you draw her in, the girl, but –
impotent – my only role is to observe. I am not able
to resist you, but yet I will not have her so destroyed.
She is too dear to me.

Claire, Sunday 16 September 1951

I guess I'd told them that it was my birthday
next weekend. They've said they'd like to take me
somewhere special. It's a celebration. For you know,
Irena said, that sixteen is a special age. They have
a friend who runs a restaurant, and that's where
they said they'd like to go. It's really awkward though.
'cos Mum and Dad had planned tea out for just
our family. I really wish that Mum and Irena
would make it up. At school when we have fights
they don't go on like this. Well, not so long.

The thing is that I really want to go with Kasals.
It just sounds so exciting. Tea out with Mum and Dad
and Paul – that's ordinary stuff. And after all,
Irena says, sixteen is very special. Their friend's Italian.
They met him on the ship that brought them
to Australia. Now he's maître d' (Irena taught me
to say that) at somewhere posh in Collins Street.

I hope that no one makes me choose. Because, you know,
I'd almost think Kasals would be my choice.

Doss, Tuesday 18 September 1951

I really think he's quite quite wrong.
I think it's all a big mistake.
Joe's pretty easy-going but I've learned
by now that when he does make
up his mind to something, I do best
to hold my peace and just agree.
But this is quite beyond a joke;
I don't know why he cannot see
this birthday invite for our child
is planned with hopes that I'll be wild.

He says that we must let her go;
they're only being very kind.
All very well for him, but then
he doesn't know how much I mind.
They've taken her away from us;
the child is only just sixteen.
For all she thinks she's worldly wise,
she's taken in by them. They've been
like spiders, and she's in their web
of influence – it's not been good.
I'd like to get them out of here,
send them away – I really would!
Our lives were simpler till they came.
I wonder if they'll ever be the same.

Claire, Sunday 23 September 1951

I won't forget this birthday. Such a strange, strange night.

When we got home, and Mum and Dad were waiting for us
in the lounge room, I knew that they expected to hear all
about it. I wasn't sure quite what to say. I told them
how the place had little candles on each table, and
statues in the hollows in the wall. I tried hard to remember
exactly what we'd eaten, even what the French words
on the menu were, but Viktor had translated what I
couldn't understand. I showed them the white flower
that he'd bought me when the flower seller came around.

I didn't tell them how Irena spent the evening dancing
with two other men they knew. Or how I'd even had a sip
of wine from Viktor's glass. I didn't say they'd ordered
a whole bottle, then another one. I somehow didn't think
Dad would have understood. Or how Viktor had tipped
the taxi driver when we got home. Dad always says
that no one should expect a tip for doing what they're
paid to do. Oh, there were lots of bits I thought
I shouldn't say. I specially didn't tell them how it felt
when Viktor danced with me. It wasn't just that I was glad
we had those lessons back at school. They were quite
different from the way he held me close. I'd never known
how that would feel. Even now, I swallow, and I feel
as if my heart is racing.

Joe, Thursday 27 September 1951

Doss packed our bags tonight.
It's a taxi to the station
early in the morning.
Train goes at eight.
Don't often take
a day off work, but then
don't often travel interstate.
The wedding's Saturday.
Doss isn't happy –
that's quite clear.
We know the Kasals
will be here, and Doss
has left a lot of food,
enough to feed an army.
But she's not certain
whether we should go.
'Come on, love,' I said
to her. 'We haven't had
a bit of time together
for a long while now.'
I think she got my meaning.
I know things have been
tough for her; she needs
a break. We both do.

Claire, Friday 28 September 1951

The lectures that they gave us! You'd think I was
a little kid. The food for every meal. What time to go to bed.
No fighting with your brother. Doing what the Kasals said.
Don't lose the front door key. Now off to school, you two.
We'll see you Sunday night. The taxi's here.

After Paul had gone, I locked the house up tight. It seemed
a long long day at school. I hardly heard a word of what
was said in classes. The others knew that Mum and Dad
had gone away. In fact Pam asked last week if I would like
to go to stay with her. I said I didn't want to leave
Paul home alone with Kasals. 'Oh, they're looking after you?'
Pam asked. 'Well, just as well his wife's there, isn't it?'
She said it nastily, so I was glad the other girls had gone
    ahead.

For just a little while, in maths, I tried to picture
what it would be like if Paul and Irena weren't there,
if in some way it was just Viktor home with me that night.
'Claire Schmidt, you're daydreaming!' Miss Albright said.
'What did I say that x would equal here?' I didn't know,
of course. I think I had another X much more in mind.

Viktor, Friday 28 September 1951

Late – but not late enough to make me sleep. I had thought,
I had hoped tonight, with Joe and Doss gone from the house,
the children safely bedded…I had thought, had hoped…
I knew it would not be, as soon as she came through the door.
'I have the headache. I am sick,' she said. Her face was white
and drawn. 'I do not eat. The woman has left food, enough
for you also. I go to bed.' We ate in silence, then they played
some card game. I could see that Claire was watching me, and so
I tried; I joined them where they played. I helped Paul
with the plane that he was building, I listened to the girl talk
of the art work she was doing. All the time my body aching,
throbbing, pounding with the thoughts that filled my day.
Slow passing hours. The time for Paul to go to bed. I knew
I would not sleep. 'I think that I will walk a while,' I said.
They know I do this often, so were not surprised.
'It's awfully cold,' said Paul, then he was gone. Claire
looked at me. 'I could come too,' she offered,
'if you'd like some company…' Her face, so hopeful,
and so young. Confiding, innocent. A moment of temptation.
So easy it would be, so comforting to have that eager body
with me, just to hold her hand and feel the tension lessen.
'A kind thought, but tonight I go alone. I am not
company tonight. You would be bored.' Her face, forlorn.
A feeling that I know so well. I felt a tenderness.
'Tomorrow we will have a special day. A holiday. We plan
it in the morning. So sleep well tonight.'

Claire, Friday 28 September 1951

He's out there walking on his own.
I should have gone.
I should be there with him.
There's something wrong.
He's not himself. Perhaps
he's worried that Irena's sick.
Perhaps there's something happened
at his work. I just know that
I want to be with him.
If only I knew how
to show him what I feel.
If only I could understand
just what it is I want.

Irena, Saturday 29 September 1951

In morning I must work – but Saturday is just half day.
Then Robert come. Two week he have not speak to me.
He take me into office. He say he take me lunch, then
afternoon we work. I know his meaning. So I say myself
'Why do this thing?' No answer come, but yet I
do as he have say, and telephone to home. The girl
surprise, then ask me, 'But you'll be home for dinner?
Viktor says we're going out.' 'Yes, yes!'

Now understand. Robert have found house for us.
Not very big, but close to city. Quick to get to,
so he say. Then look at me. 'When cat's away…'
he say. I do not understand. But inside self I do.

All afternoon I think. But to have house. To leave behind
that room. Is worth the price. The cost no matter.

At night we sit at dinner. They have had good day, and all
that they have see they tell. Aquarium, with fish.
I glad I not there. Fish are stupid creatures. *Dümkopf!*
My mother call them. Swimming all day round in circle.
No life in fish. My mother was wise woman. So why
I go in circle, back with Robert? Am I fish?

I think that Viktor know. He watch me all through meal,
and drink much wine. In taxi on way home Paul soon asleep,
but not the girl. She look at Viktor, then at me, then out
through window. No one speak. We drive. No words.

I go to room, and Viktor follow. 'Pah!' I say.
'You smell of drink. I do not want you touch me.'
His face like sad dog at the door. 'So why not me?'
he ask. Then I know that he know.

Claire, Saturday 29 September 1951

It was such a happy day, even though Irena had to work.
Viktor really tried so hard to make it all quite perfect.
It was. I can't work out just what it was made everything go wrong.
I think it started with Irena coming home. They didn't really
speak. In fact he didn't look at her all night. I tried to talk
at dinner, because the silence was quite awful. Even Paul
could feel it. I think that in the taxi coming home
he just pretended he had gone to sleep. We said good night
politely, thanked Viktor for a lovely day, told him the restaurant
had been real nice. Then we went off as quickly
as we could. This hasn't been the way I'd pictured it.
I just can't get to sleep; my tummy's knotted up
and everything feels wrong. I don't think Viktor's
sleeping either. Either that, or someone's left the lamp on
in the lounge room. I'd better turn it off. And maybe
get a glass of milk. Mum always says that helps you
get to sleep. Perhaps if he's still up, he'd like one too.
I want to be the one to comfort him.

Viktor, Saturday 29 September, 1951

So desolation grows. Was it for this that we came here?
So much we have endured, in hope of better life.
I could not call this better. I know what you have done.
There is no need to ask, or you to say. Yet still,
in spite of all, I need you with such desperation.
So long it has been. Now here, in this half light,
I can imagine that you come to me, take from my grasp
the glass, and draw me to you, guide my hand into
your secret parts, lay your lips on mine, and take me
to your bed.
Irena.
As my breathing quickens, I can feel you here.

For one brief moment, when the door is opened
a woman's figure enters. My heart lifts.
But then I see it is not you. It's Claire.
She comes close to me, sits; I feel the warmth
of all that firm young flesh. It burns into my mind,
and can obliterate the thoughts of you.
'You're sad,' she says to me. 'I wish that
I could help.' She nestles close. I find my arm
move round her with no willing on my part. We sit
in silence, and I clench my fist to keep it still.
But as my body stirs, I find my voice, though
even to my ears it sounds so strange.
'It is too late. You need to go to bed.'
She turns to me. 'I just can't get to sleep tonight.
When I was little, and I couldn't sleep, sometimes
my dad would tuck me in. That helped.
Maybe I'd sleep if you would tuck me in...'

Dear God, where has she learned this? But I
find myself drawing her upright, walking with her
like a sleepwalker towards the room,
not knowing what will be. We reach the door;
inside the bed is waiting, together we move to it.
She slides between the sheets, and lifts her face
to me in invitation. 'Kiss me goodnight?' she asks.
I bend towards her; in that moment there is promise
of so much. So much I need and yearn for.
In that kiss there is, for her, awakening.

And for me.

I rise. I turn. I hear my strangled voice.
'Sleep well. Good night.'

Claire, Sunday 30 September 1951

My face is burning up.
I feel quite sick with shame.
What if Mum and Dad find out?
What if he tells them
I asked him to my room?
I can't bear to think
any more about it.
What did I do?
What did I say?
I'll never look at him again.
I hate him.
I can't imagine
what I thought
would happen.
But not that.
So horrible.
I felt his tongue
between my lips.
Disgusting.
Is this what grown-ups do?
The taste of wine.
I never want to see his face again.

Yet it was exciting.
I couldn't breathe.
The feeling that it gave me,
something I'd never felt before.

But what if he had stayed…

But what if Mum and Dad find out?

And later on the sounds that came
from their room opposite.
I put my hands over my ears.
I did not want to hear.

Was it his kiss
I did not like?

Or was it that
he didn't stay?

Joe, Tuesday 2 October 1951

At first Doss didn't want
to say what Claire had told her.
We knew that there
was something wrong
as soon as we got home.
Paul said his sister had been sick
and stayed in bed all day.
A good kid, Paul.
He made her sandwiches.
Viktor had gone out.
Where was Irena?'
I asked Paul.
'Dunno,' he said.
'We didn't see her
much at all.'

Doss was firm.
'That's it, Joe.
End of week
they leave!'
'You can't just
throw them out,'
I told her, but
when she said that
Viktor had been in
Claire's room in the night,
I saw red too.
'No, nothing happened.'

She was quick to tell me
that. 'But, Joe,
it's not the point.
It's really what
it could have been.
They've got to go.'

I can't believe it.
He's a decent cove.
But then Claire wouldn't
make a story like that up.

Doss, Thursday 4 October 1951

I really would have wanted Joe
to tell him what we thought
of someone who would so
abuse our trust. I think he ought
have laid it on the line –
that's not Joe's way.
'But nothing happened, Doss.'
He thinks that if we say
too much we only make
things worse. 'It must be hell
for someone, hooked up to
a bitch like that. You can tell
what he's been through.'
I was surprised. That's not a word
that you too often hear Joe use.
In fact, I've hardly ever heard
that word from him. It goes to show
just how upset he's been.
In any case, they are about to go –
turns out Irena's boss has found
a house that they can cheaply rent.
Good timing! is all I can say;
it really is quite heaven sent.

Viktor, Saturday 6 October 1951

What to say? I wish so much that I could tell Joe
words that never can be said. I would not harm
your daughter Joe. I think he knows
the truth of that. But not his wife. She will not
look at me. Nor Claire. She leaves a room if I come in.
If there is damage done, I wish I could undo.

But worse, the damage she has done to me.

I wonder if Irena knows. I think about that night,
the night I came to her and forced her, stopped up
all her cries, her protests, took her as I wanted.
All the anguish of these months of waiting,
all my need, the flooding of my body with desire,
the fierce exultant passion as I took her.
She belonged to me.

But where the satisfaction? None in that. A coupling
of two animals, the stronger on the top. Bile rises
in my mouth when I think of her body, tense,
resistant, under me. Now she looks at me in fear.
I am lessened by what I have done.

Let her tell him that –
how the brute, her husband, raped her in the night.
But even while I took her, even with the shame
a fierce pleasure that I'd shown her she was mine.
It is my payment for the house.
Tomorrow, when we move into his house,
she will know that he is not the only one she pays.

Doss, Sunday 7 October 1951

Well Lizzie, I know that you're not surprised
to find they're gone. You always thought
it wouldn't work. I guess you recognised
it's better if we keep to our own sort.
He really seemed a chap who was OK
although you always seemed to wonder –
in fact I think I've even heard you say
you weren't too sure that maybe even under
all his polish he might be two-faced.

Now I can see why you could feel some doubt
but take my word for it, it's quite misplaced.
I tell you nothing's funny about
the way they left. They'd found another place to live –
although I'm not denying I was glad to see them go.
Now Liz, we're friends from way back – please don't give
me any more about the way it's been with them, so
we don't spoil a friendship. We've got back Claire…
at least I hope the girl will soon forget
the things she's learned from them, and all their
foreign ways, and be our child again. But yet
I can't help wondering about it all because
I'm not too sure how easy that will be.
Although I've put the house straight just the way it was,
the future's something only time will let us see.

Claire, Monday 8 October 1951

It seems so long since I have been here –
back in my own room.
They've gone.
It's almost as if they were never here.
Mum spent all yesterday on cleaning.
It was as if she tried to make it all
the way it was before. Not that there was
too much left over from their stay.
At least, it didn't seem that way at first…
Mum put my pictures back, and told me that
she'd take Irena's curtains down.
But I said no. I really want to make my room
the way Irena had it. It was better.

I found it in the top drawer,
a little bottle of her perfume. I felt sad.
I thought about the things that she had showed me,
how their lives had been. I thought how life
could be. I put her perfume on,
pretended that I was Irena. What it might be like
if I became Irena. 'Cos this is what I want –
I know it now. I want to be Irena.

And then I think of him. I swallow hard.
It hurts.

In spite of all the cleaning yesterday, this isn't
my old room. Mum said I can stay home
from school today. I'm looking peaky –
that's her word for it whenever we are sick.
She brought me breakfast on a tray – she'd even
made egg soldiers, and it made me want to cry.
I thought of how I'd loved them when I was
a little kid. Seems quite a long time back.
Made me remember all the years she'd been
my Mum and taken care of me when I was sick.
But that's all past. She came to get the tray.
For just a minute – when I saw her face,
the way it sort of crumpled when she saw
I hadn't eaten anything – I almost called her back
to say that I was sorry. But I wasn't sure what for.

Somewhere I hear the vacuum cleaner going,
but here in bed I'm listening to another sound –
Mum has the wireless on, and Perry Como's singing –
perhaps it's Nat King Cole – it's hard to hear, but
I can tell the song. He's singing 'Blue Moon'
and it's sad.

It seems a bit wrong too, when up there on the wall
I see the peaches, just the way they always were.

Claire, 2009

But they were not the same – and even then,
child that I was, I knew it. They would never
be the same. There is no going back
to innocence, no matter how we try.

And when have I been innocent? All life
is one long series of betrayals. Little guilts
or large – they may be light or heavy on the scale
but they will always weigh it down.
I look back through the years. Strange how one
never sees the pattern till the picture's finished –
the last piece in the jigsaw, then it's clear.

Hard to think back to what I was, that child.
An innocent? Let's have no self-delusions.
Even then I knew what I was doing.
But to run from it, try to scurry back
to childhood, quell that quivering excitement
of the body…did I really think I could?

Betrayal? What did I betray? Just him?
Or so much more?

The other faces crowd in on me from the years.
They swim beneath the boat, and clamour
for me, asking what? Too late to make amends.
Is recognition any recompense?

And what would it have been, had I not
made my choices, re-defined myself, and
taken on the patterns of another world?
Decisions lightly made, and others that cost more.

The unborn child who could have been…
The unborn child who should have been!
At least my parents never knew that choice I'd made.

Irena…am I you indeed?
I see again the girl who said,
'I want the life that you have shown me.'
And now I see also that I am you.
My parents stand before me –
their ageing faces so confused, disturbed, rejected –
deeply hurt. A pattern started;
a new road chosen, but the one not chosen
always lingering in the mind, behind that mesh
of guilt.

I gave them what I could. The academic honours
that he valued, success, a public reputation,
a life that she could boast of, even if not share.
So when they looked at me, why did I feel
the accusation in their eyes? Why did they look
betrayed?

Claire, Blues Interlude 3

Somewhere in the night a child is crying.
Somewhere in the blackness of the night a child is crying bitter tears.
Scorching searing tears that never seem to end.

   Rudderless and floating,
   seas around me higher,
   days spin into days,
   nights bring fever fire.
   Clocks tick madly on,
   water runs uphill,
   stars go wheeling by,
   while the earth stands still.

Then memories come to score my heart.
Then memories with their fingernails scratch score lines in my heart.
The ashes of the day, a breeding ground for night-time tears.

   Cacophony of sounds
   fills the screaming air.
   Skulls leap from the graves
   but there's no one there.
   Rats' breath hangs in clouds,
   eyelids glue together.
   aged crones watch me die
   choking on a feather.

Nightmares come when all the world is quiet.
Haunting nightmares come when all the velvet world is quiet in the darkness.
They shroud me with the grave cloths of the life I never gave a chance.

Claire, 2009

I saw him only once after the day they left.
It was a long time after. I walked, not really
looking where I went, down Collins Street.
A rainy afternoon, and scurrying crowds.
Pavements wet and slippery, umbrellas
flapping in a gusty wind. And in the gutters
grimy scraps caught sodden in the scum.
The detritus of living. I'd come out from
warmth and golden light – another small café –
not memorable; I'd said my last goodbyes to one
more failed entanglement, and moved
dispiritedly out into the cold. I brushed
against a small dark man, and knew at once
it was the figure from my dreams. But yet
not so. Diminished. Beaten. Shoulders hunched,
and not against the cold. He raised his hat,
yes even now, still hat, still courteous,
but did not look at me. 'Pardon!' he said,
and hurried on.

He did not know me. Not surprising, after all
these years. And yet I knew him instantly;
his face has been the backdrop to my dreams
so many nights. The nightmares too.
'Pardon!' he said. Oh, Viktor, if you only knew
how many times I would have said that word to you!

Claire, 2009

She clatters back into the room. I would have thought
with what I'm paying here, they would at least
get staff who could afford soft shoes. But no,
again we get the smile – professional, impersonal –
I would not have it any other way. A life that's spent
avoiding such connections should not now
in times of fear expect it to be different.

'Do you need anything?'

I snap. I snarl. It is my way.
They would not know me if I softened.
What is more,
I would not know myself.

'Nothing you can give me!'

A truthful answer, but she leaves affronted.

I think about my tombstone, and the word
that I have chosen for it. Some will look,
and contemplate the possibility that
in the end I have sought mercy from above.
Not so. That one word 'Pardon' is my plea
to all those down the years, the sea of faces,
those who haunt my dreams. Guilt ridden,
I turn, as is my wont, to words
from bygone times, in recognition there are acts
for which forgiveness never comes. So many,
in the life I chose to live. The faces are indeed
a multitudinous sea. In words of others
I find what I now feel. 'Incarnadined?' The sea?

Macbeth too knew the word. My dreams are haunted
not with blood, but with the thousand small betrayals
that have been my life.

And while I wait, I still see golden peaches on the wall.
They too are meaningless. I watch them as they lessen;
the sun moves upward through the sky – their fullness fades,
reduces. First three-quarters, then a half,
and now a quarter circle. Soon they will be gone.
Soon all will go.